RESILIENCE

VENGEANCE AND VAMPIRES BOOK TWO

ALICIA RADES

Published by Crystallite Publishing LLC.
Produced in the United States of America.
Edited by Megan Linski.
Cover design by KnesArt.

For the fighter in all of us.

1

M atias Vayne must've had a dick the size of a breath mint. That was the only explanation I could think of as I stood at the base of Vayne Tower, trying to take in its sheer magnitude. This vamp was definitely compensating for something.

The morning sun was hidden behind the clouds—or was it smog?—but still, the windows six hundred feet above my head seemed to reflect the light. It wasn't the tallest building in Chicago, but it certainly stood out in the forest of skyscrapers with its clean, modern architecture.

"Rae?" Venn's voice cut through my thoughts.

I tore my gaze from the massive structure and turned to him. He wore a navy button-down collared shirt over a clean white t-shirt and a pair of jeans. The sleeves were rolled up casually, showing off his toned forearms. His dark eyes traveled over me, sending a wave of butterflies to dance around in my stomach. I swore Venn got hotter by the day.

So unfair.

"Are you ready?" he asked.

"Yeah," I said. "I just didn't think it'd be... so big."

"I know," Ryland agreed from several paces ahead. "It's a little over-the-top, isn't it?"

"Maybe he needs it," Teagan mumbled. "You know, for his... ego."

Fiona stifled a laugh beside Teagan. She wore black slacks and a nice purple top, but she didn't have the heels for it. Teagan hadn't foregone her usual skin-tight cargo pants, but she'd put an olive-green cardigan over her black tank top and let her dark hair fall in waves around her shoulders.

After fleeing their burning home, none of us had many personal items with us anymore. Teagan, Venn, and Fiona had managed to pack a few bags in the car before the fire consumed everything else, but Ryland and I had nothing. I still wore my ripped jeans, black tee, and boots. Ryland wore his usual enchanted clothing—jeans and a t-shirt. His left arm hung in a sling we'd picked up this morning, since the bones were still healing after the vampire attack.

Even with everyone else's attempt to look business-casual, we still stuck out in the sea of businessmen and women rushing to their next appointments. Luckily, most people didn't notice us. They were either preoccupied on their phones or staring straight ahead like robots. I had the urge to slap one of them just to see if they had feelings.

I already missed Nocton, where we only had a hundred thousand people or so to worry about. Cities packed to the millions weren't exactly my thing. But I had to face it for a few hours, because once we got inside and exchanged the Leora Locket for Sondra's safety, we'd finally be able to hunt down my sister.

As we approached the front doors, Fiona leaned over to me and whispered. "You're going to love Sondra. She once made Ryland believe he was a chicken for three days because he insulted her drawings. We fed him dry cereal just to watch him peck at it."

She giggled, lightening the mood. I couldn't help but laugh at the thought.

We stepped into a huge lobby. Tile floor stretched out in front of us, and the room bustled with foot traffic. The ceiling was so high and the room so long that I was pretty sure it was big enough to play football in. The tall windows were heavily tinted, blocking out most of the sun and casting a gray hue across the room. I noticed several pairs of silver eyes and realized the dark windows provided enough sun protection to allow vampires to roam the building during the day.

The lobby was empty of everything—even color—except for a long white desk situated opposite the door. There weren't even any seating areas—or God forbid, a plant. Eight elevators lined the wall beside the front desk, where people hurried in and out of them.

Ryland led the way across the lobby and stopped at the front desk. A thin woman in a dark blazer looked up from her computer. Her lips immediately turned down, showing the age lines around her eyes that she clearly tried to hide.

"Can I help you?" She sounded like she meant it, but there was judgement in her eyes. Apparently, we didn't look rich enough for her blood. She probably thought we were lost and needed directions or something.

"Yes," Ryland said in a confident tone. "We're here to see Matias Vayne."

The woman couldn't hide the scoff that escaped her lips. Her expression quickly fell so that I could barely read her face. Another robot. We wouldn't want genuine human interaction, would we?

No, I thought, *not when you work with heartless vamps.*

"I'm sorry," Robot Lady said, "but Mr. Vayne doesn't take walk-ins."

"He will for us," Ryland insisted. "Tell him we're here on behalf of Leora."

"I'm sorry," she repeated, "but your boss is going to have to call Mr. Vayne's secretary privately to set up an appointment."

I held my breath. We *had* to get in. There was no way we were leaving here without Sondra.

I wasn't going to wait around. I pushed past Ryland and leaned my elbows against the counter. "You have a phone right there. Call his office and let him know we're here."

"Ma'am," she said with a frown, like my demand only amused her, "if I called Mr. Vayne every time someone came in asking for him, he'd never get any work done. If this is an urgent matter, your boss can—"

"Is there a problem here?" A woman with flawless dark skin and silver eyes stepped forward. Even her vampirism couldn't strip away her dark skin tone. Her hair was pulled back into a tight bun at the base of her neck, and she wore a slimming red pantsuit and high heels.

"They want to see Mr. Vayne," Robot Lady replied. "On behalf of... what did you say your boss's name was?"

"Leora," Ryland told her.

"Right. And I told them—" Robot Lady started, but the vampire cut her off.

"Leora?" She looked at us in shock. "Please, come with me."

Robot Lady stared at us with her mouth agape as we followed behind her vampire boss. She led us away from the long line of elevators and to a hall at the far end of the lobby.

"Mr. Vayne has been eagerly awaiting your arrival," she said in a professional tone.

"We apologize that we couldn't make it sooner," Fiona said.

Vampire Boss stopped at the end of the hall and pressed a button beside the lone elevator that stood there. She folded her hands and turned to us. "Not to worry. You're here now, and that's what's important."

The elevator doors slid open, and Vampire Boss gestured for us to step inside. We all filed in. She pressed the button to the top floor, and the doors glided shut.

My gut twisted as the elevator ascended, and it wasn't because I was scared of cramped spaces. We'd just locked ourselves in a tiny room with a vampire who could eat us all if she wanted to. Not that she'd succeed, considering she was outnumbered, but I still felt uneasy in her presence. Instinct told me to stake a weapon through her heart, but even if it came to that, there were no weapons in the immediate vicinity. We'd all agreed Teagan should leave her blades in the car so we wouldn't provoke the vamps.

The elevator was eerily quiet, despite the tacky music playing softly from hidden speakers. Venn must've noticed my unease, because he grabbed my hand and squeezed it. Tingles spread across my skin at his touch. I laced my fingers through his and squeezed back.

The elevator doors opened, revealing an elegant waiting room. There were no windows, and the room was cast in soft lighting. Black carpet stretched from one gray wall to the other. Plush red couches that looked worth more than I made in a year sat around a burning gas fireplace. If Matias was going for *modern vampire lair*, he'd certainly hit the decor on the nose.

Beyond the waiting area, a blonde woman with breasts that bulged out of her top sat behind a long reception desk. She wore a pair of reading glasses, but I knew she didn't need them. Her silver eyes gave her away as a vampire. Along with flawless beauty and supernatural strength, vampires had perfect vision. Beside Blondie and straight across from the elevator sat a pair of double doors.

Blondie glanced up from her desk and smiled when she saw Vampire Boss leading us into the room. "What can I help you with, Veronica?"

"These ladies and gentlemen are here to see Mr. Vayne," Vampire Boss—Veronica—replied, stopping at the desk.

Blondie turned to her computer. "Do they have an appointment?"

"No, which is why I escorted them here personally," Veronica said. "They're here on behalf of Leora."

Blondie typed something into her computer. "Mm... Leora... I don't think—" Realization suddenly dawned. "Oh! I'll let Mr. Vayne know right away." Blondie quickly picked up the phone on her desk and punched in a number.

"Please, sit," Veronica offered, gesturing to the red chairs nearby. "Can I get you anything while you wait?"

I could've asked for a water, but who knew if they served anything but blood around here? They probably planned to add us to the menu.

"No, thanks," Venn said. "We're fine."

Everyone else nodded in agreement.

"Enjoy your visit to Vayne Tower," Veronica said kindly before leaving us alone and returning to the elevator.

Because I was *so* going to enjoy myself in a vampire-infested skyscraper.

I shifted uncomfortably in my seat. For expensive-looking couches, they weren't very comfortable.

"You okay?" Venn asked from beside me.

I nodded, though honestly, I felt uneasy. I preferred to kick vampire ass on the street, where there was an easy escape. Here, we were trapped. I hoped Ryland knew what he was doing.

From the chair beside Venn, Fiona grabbed a magazine off the end table and began flipping through it. Teagan sat close to her, looking distressed. Ryland stood near the fireplace with a hard look on his face. He wasn't about to try getting comfortable in a place like this.

Venn's thigh brushed against mine. My skin heated where he touched me, and all I wanted to do was scoot closer to him and wrap my arms around him. Freaking hormones. Now was not the time.

We were only alone for a moment before the double doors beside the reception desk swung open. I turned to see a man in his early forties step out of the room. He had a strong jaw, straight nose, and a five o'clock shadow that most women would swoon over. Like all vampires, his skin was flawless, and his eyes were silver. He wore a dark tailored suit that showed off his trim figure. Not a single one of his brown hairs was misplaced. Everything about him screamed *money*. Though the very sight of the vampire repulsed me, I couldn't deny that the guy was insanely attractive. What was it with rich, attractive men like him? He set off all sorts of *asshole* alarms.

I stood, mostly because I didn't want to let my guard down, but I suspected Venn, Teagan, and Fiona followed suit out of respect.

"Ryland," the vampire sang. He opened his arms wide, as if expecting a hug.

Ryland stood rigid. "Matias."

Matias dropped his arms. Up close, I got a better look at his eyes. I could've sworn I recognized him from somewhere.

I racked my brain trying to remember, but I figured I'd just seen him in a TV commercial or something.

Matias's eyes scanned our group until they fell on me. "Who's the lovely new lady?"

He reached out his hand for mine. I swallowed hard but let him take it. This guy probably wiped his ass with hundred-dollar bills. I didn't want to find out what he'd use his money for if we disrespected him. His fingers were cold, sending a shiver down my spine. He brought my hand to his face and brushed his icy lips across it. I wanted to gag.

Venn stepped forward. "This is Rae, and if you know what's good for you, you'll keep your grubby little hands off of her."

Matias dropped my hand. Venn was officially my hero. I could kiss him right now. Then again, I always wanted to kiss him.

"I think the witch-shifter can speak for herself," Matias said, eyeing me curiously.

"I can," I replied through tight lips. "But you're lucky I didn't. How'd you know I was a witch?"

Matias smirked. "I didn't, but you've just confirmed it."

"You play dirty. I see how it is," I said.

Matias laughed. "Sweetheart, I'm a vampire. Dirty is all we know. I may be able to find a position here for you if you're in to that kind of thing."

Was he hitting on me? *Gross!*

Venn snuck his shoulder in front of mine protectively. Good thing, because if Matias kept looking at me that way, my knee would be all up in his royal jewels. My lack of self-control was a serious curse.

"Are we done yet?" Ryland cut in. He sounded completely

unamused. "Let's cut to the chase, Matias. You know why we're here."

Matias's eyes lit up. "Yes, of course. I presume you have the item on you."

The way he said it suggested the family wouldn't dare enter this building without it.

"We want to see Sondra first," Ryland demanded.

"You'll see her as soon as I receive the locket," Matias said coolly.

"No," Teagan protested.

"I've got this, Tea," Ryland said under his breath as he placed a hand on her shoulder.

Teagan ignored him. "You'll bring her out here safe and unharmed, or you can kiss your precious locket goodbye."

Matias smirked, like he found Teagan amusing. He glanced between the five of us and must've decided we weren't screwing around.

"Fair enough." Matias turned to Blondie behind her desk. "Allison, call Walker and tell him to bring the girl."

"Yes, sir," Allison said as she picked up the phone on her desk.

The following silence was agonizing. Matias stood there with his hands folded in front of him. He held his head high, looking positively pleased. Though Ryland held his gaze, Matias's eyes kept flickering toward me. It made my skin crawl.

The sound of a door opening across the room caught all of our attention. A tall, muscular vampire in a suit stepped into room, dragging a woman by her wrist behind him.

"Let me go!" she protested.

"Do as she says, Walker," Matias commanded calmly. "She is, after all, our guest."

Walker dropped the woman's hand, and she straightened. She was tall, but so thin that it looked like they hadn't fed her in days. She looked at least thirty, and though she had dark circles under her brown eyes and wore no makeup, she was beautiful. Her facial structure was similar to Fiona's, but her chestnut hair matched Ryland's.

I couldn't explain it, but I could sense a goodness radiating off of her, like she was someone I could trust even though she was a complete stranger.

Her eyes fell on our group, and she instantly rushed forward.

"Hold on, Sondra." Matias held a hand up, and Sondra stopped in her tracks.

"What'd you do to her?" Venn demanded.

Matias shrugged. "Nothing. It's not my fault she refused to eat. I'll take the locket now."

"Do we have your word that we'll be allowed to leave unharmed?" Ryland asked.

"Yes," Matias answered. "I'm a vampire. I'm not a monster. I run clean business deals."

A muscle popped in Ryland's jaw. I wasn't sure how Matias could consider a hostage situation a *clean* business deal.

Matias held out his hand expectantly, and Ryland reached into his pocket and pulled out the golden locket. He placed it in Matias's hand.

"It's been a pleasure doing business with you," Matias said with a smile. "Half of the agreed amount will be deposited into your bank account within the hour."

"Half?" Ryland gawked.

"Yes, half." Matias was dead serious. "You were late on your delivery. Be glad I'm generous enough to offer payment at all, considering your unprofessionalism."

Nobody said anything. I mean, Matias was right. He could've just had his vampire staff kill us all. Matias turned on his heel. Sondra ran forward, and Fiona pushed past the rest of us to reach her first. They fell into an embrace. Fiona buried her face in Sondra's hair.

"I'm so glad you're all okay," Sondra whispered.

Teagan stepped forward and joined in their hug. Venn stayed back and wrapped an arm around my waist. I leaned into him, welcoming his comfort.

Ryland cleared his throat and stole a glance at Matias, who'd stopped in front of the double doors to watch us. *Creep.*

"A lot has happened since you've been gone," Ryland said.

Sondra caught my eye. She tilted her head, as if trying to recall where she'd seen me before. I wondered if maybe she'd visited Bloodstone, the spell shop I worked at—used to work at.

"I can see that," she said. "I'm Sondra, but I guess you knew that already."

I shook the hand she offered and nodded.

"We can get to more formal introductions later," Venn said. "Let's get you somewhere comfortable."

"Agreed," Sondra said quickly.

Matias's eyes followed us all the way to the elevator. Every time I looked back, he was staring at me. Shivers tickled down my spine like a thousand tiny spiders crawling across my back. I itched for him to give me a reason to pick a fight. The guy was pompous as hell. Every instinct told me to run far, far away.

Or punch him in the nose. One of the two.

Venn must've noticed my discomfort, because he pulled me closer. "It's okay. We'll be out of here soon enough."

We filed into the elevator, and I whispered to Venn under my breath. "That guy creeps me out."

"I know," Venn agreed. "He creeps everyone out."

The hair on the back of my neck rose as we exited the building. It was as if Matias's eyes were still on me. Normally, vampires didn't scare me, but in that moment, an all-consuming fear hit my chest like a freight train. What if he *was* watching me?

"What do you think he's going to use the Leora Locket for?" I asked. I knew it could be used to tell the future based on a person's current intentions, but I couldn't help but wonder what his end goal was. Did he want the locket as a novelty item, or was there something bigger going on here?

"It doesn't matter," Fiona said as we descended the steps in front of Vayne Tower. "I told you it's pretty useless anyway."

"It depends on how you use it," Sondra mumbled under her breath.

"What do you mean?" Teagan asked.

Sondra hesitated and glanced around at the bustling street. "I have something to tell all of you, but we need to find some-where safe to talk. I don't think—" Sondra cut off.

"Think what?" Venn asked.

"Does anyone else feel that?" Sondra whispered while quickening her step.

Ryland looked around to follow Sondra's flickering gaze. He glanced to the darkening sky. "Feel what? A storm rolling in?"

"No," Sondra said. "That tingle on the back of your neck, like—"

"Like you're being watched?" I cut in.

Sondra swallowed. "Exactly. We need to get to the car now. I think we're being followed."

2

———

"What the hell's going on?" Ryland demanded the second we were back in the car.

Fiona shifted into her fox form and curled up on Sondra's lap next to me in the back seat. It was the only way we'd all fit. Venn sat on my other side with his comforting arm around me. It helped slow my pounding heart that had followed me on the long walk back to the car.

Teagan turned in the passenger seat to face us. "They didn't hurt you, did they?"

"No," Sondra said in a rush. "Just start the car, and let's get out of here."

Ryland turned the key and shifted into drive. I had no idea where he was headed. I only knew that none of us wanted to hang around Vayne Tower. As soon as we were moving, I felt like I could finally breathe again. The tingle on the back of my neck had vanished, but there was still a feeling in the pit of my stomach that told me I shouldn't let my guard down just yet.

"So, Sondra, about Rae…" Venn started.

"We can talk about what happened while I was gone later,"

13

Sondra insisted. "Right now, we have more pressing matters. I overheard some things. I know why Matias wanted the locket. We have to stop him."

Every muscle in my body tensed.

Ryland glanced to Sondra in the rearview mirror. "I thought you said this was a harmless job. You said he wouldn't even know how to use the locket."

"And I also said the locket's power lies in how you use it," Sondra clarified. "I thought for sure he was going to use it to watch his competitors. The locket only shows a *possible* future. It's very hard to use it to predict someone else's intentions."

Ryland pressed the brakes as the cars in front of us slowed at a stoplight. "What's he going to use it for, then?"

"He's not going to use it to predict someone else's intentions," Sondra said. "He's going to use it to predict his own."

My brow furrowed. Did she mean he was going to use it to gamble?

"What does that even mean?" Teagan asked.

Sondra swallowed. "He's going to use the locket to predict the outcome of his decisions so that he can find the thing he really wants."

"Which is...?" Venn prodded.

"He just called it the Artifact," Sondra answered. "From what I heard, it's an ancient object that's been hidden for centuries that's capable of wiping out magic again—for everyone except the owner."

"Wait," I blurted, my whole body igniting in alarm. "Matias wants to be the *only* person who can use magic?"

Pompous ass.

Sondra nodded.

"That doesn't make any sense," Teagan pointed out. "He's a vampire. How's he going to use magic?"

"I don't know," Sondra admitted. "He could retrieve the artifact now and wait for reincarnation. That's what I'd do."

"Hold up," I stopped her. "Reincarnation?"

Why hadn't anyone mentioned this to me when they told me about Synchrony?

"Yes, reincarnation," Sondra confirmed. "It's the only reason Matias hired us to find the locket in the first place."

I stared at her, completely baffled.

"Sondra was the witch who created the Leora Locket," Venn explained.

"I thought the Leora Locket was centuries old," I said. "And Fiona told me the witch who created it was named Leora."

"Yes," Sondra agreed. "That was my name, in a past life."

I pressed my fingers to my temples. Holy crap! Past lives? It was a lot to wrap my head around, though I shouldn't have been surprised by anything these days.

I lifted my head, my curiosity piqued. "How'd you create it?"

Sondra glanced to Venn, as if wondering how much I already knew and how much she could trust me to share.

"Magic can be bound to everyday objects," Venn explained. "It usually happens over time when an object is long associated with strong emotions, which could be good or bad. That's why houses can be haunted or a rabbit's foot can bring luck. Things like family heirlooms or old wedding rings tend to have a lot of positive magic tied to them. A weapon used in murder would have a lot of bad energy surrounding it."

I shuddered thinking about it.

"That's not the only way to create a magical object," Sondra said. "Witches can infuse magic into things, such as by using them in a powerful spell. For most people, these magical artifacts will affect their emotions, depending on the energy they give off. For witches, they can be incredibly valuable. They can be used in certain spells or can amplify a witch's abilities. They can be very dangerous if the wrong witch gets their hands on them."

"When you say you created the Leora Locket in a past life and found it in this one… you just remembered where you left it?" I asked. "And if Matias finds the Artifact in this life, he'll remember in his next?"

Sondra shook her head. "It's not that easy. As a high witch, I'm able to remember bits and pieces of my past lives, but they're not as strong as my memories of this life. The memories come to me in in flashes or in dreams. It took us months of gathering clues from visions of my past life to find the locket."

"So, Matias would have to be born a high witch in his next life to even have a chance of using the Artifact?" I asked, relaxing slightly.

Sondra frowned. "That's not how it works. You aren't born a witch by chance."

What she said completely shocked me. If I wasn't a witch by chance, how did I become one?

"Excuse me?" I asked.

"Witch magic is connected to your soul," Teagan told me. "It's all about how closely connected you are to Synchrony. If you were a witch in a past life, you're more likely to be a witch in the next life. You don't get to become a high witch without lifetimes of practice under your belt. That's why, even though the rest of us understand magic, none of us are any good at it… yet. But we're all working on it."

"Anyone can become a witch?" I asked.

"Yes," Sondra confirmed. "The ability can be nurtured. The more a person studies witchcraft throughout their lives, the more powerful he or she becomes. It's easier with each life-time. I think Matias used to be a witch before he became a vampire. It makes sense how he accomplished so much in the business world."

My head spun. "I'm guessing you know why vampires can't use witch magic. You seem to know everything else."

"Vampires are ruthless because the vampire virus damages their soul," Sondra explained. "But since witch magic is connected to the soul, they're unable to access magic. No one's quite sure how badly vampirism damages the soul, but I think that when a vampire dies, their soul is freed from their body's prison, and they start over in a new life."

"Killing them is doing them a favor," Ryland mumbled from the driver's seat.

Huh. You learn something new every day.

"Why don't all vampires want to die, then?" I asked.

"Because they don't all believe the same thing," Teagan answered. "And they don't want to lose their immortality. They'd lose any power they've already established and have to start over. Which makes me think Matias isn't going to wait around to be reincarnated to use this artifact. He's so rich, he could easily pay a witch to do it for him."

"Why would he do that?" I asked.

Teagan shrugged. "I can think of a lot of reasons. Maybe he wants to eliminate some of his competition. My guess is that he wants to control magic and sell it to the highest bidder."

Venn turned to Sondra. "Would this artifact allow him to do that?"

"It sounded like it," she replied. "I think that's what makes it so powerful, that the owner gets to pick and choose who keeps their magic and who doesn't."

"That's pure evil!" I blurted. "So essentially he'd be the most powerful man alive?" *And the richest, too.*

Who the hell did he think he was, trying to strip everyone of their magic? No more healing spells from me. No more shifting into a raven. No more super strength so I could protect humans against vampires. It felt like a personal attack. I shook in rage.

"No kidding," Sondra agreed. "That's why we have to go after it and destroy it. No one should have that kind of power."

Ryland's good hand tightened around the steering wheel. "We should've killed him back there."

"If we killed him, then what?" Sondra asked. "We'd just walk out of Vayne Tower? We all would've been executed on the spot. If the chance presents itself, believe me, I'll be the first to drive a stake through his heart."

Sondra was fierce. I liked her.

"Why couldn't you have escaped?" I blurted. "I mean, if you're a high witch."

Sondra sighed. "First of all, Matias's place is heavily enchanted. Second, even high witches have their limits."

Ryland floored the pedal as we turned onto the freeway ramp. "What if he uses the locket to watch us? He's at a huge advantage here."

"I know," Sondra admitted. "I haven't figured that part out yet. Either way, we have to find this thing before he does."

My jaw clenched. What about the promise Venn made to me?

"We're just going to drop everything to go after it?" I tried to keep the irritation out of my tone, but I couldn't help it.

"It's not like we have anything to go back to," Teagan mumbled.

Sondra sat straighter. "What do you mean?"

Everyone exchanged a glance. Fiona dropped her head. It was clear no one knew how to tell her.

Teagan's fingers tightened against the back of her seat. "I'm going to be blunt, because there's no other way to tell you... the house burnt down."

"What?!" Sondra exploded. She seemed like such a quiet, gentle person that it surprised me to hear her shout.

"We had a run-in with Maliya," Venn admitted. "She came to the house and... it was the only way we could escape. We were kind of hoping everyone would presume us dead in the fire."

Sondra pressed two fingers to her eyes. "It's okay," she finally said with a sigh. "What matters is that none of you were hurt."

"Where do we start?" Venn asked.

The breath left my chest. I stared at him in shock. He was just going to ignore his promise to me?

Of course—because he'd known these people a heck of a lot longer than he knew me. Why would he feel any loyalty toward me? Plus, it only made sense to go after the thing that would save a bunch of people rather than going after one person who may or may not still be alive.

She's alive, I told myself. *And I finally have a lead. I just didn't want to do this alone.*

I turned my gaze from Venn, hoping he wouldn't notice my expression. I couldn't tell him what I was really thinking. It was selfish.

"I want to stop for supplies," Sondra said. "Remember my friend Amalia? She helped us with a job last year. She lives here in Chicago and can help us get what we need. I'll run a spell that should help us figure out where to start. And for heaven's sake, can we please stop for a burger or something? I'm starving."

Venn pulled me closer and whispered in my ear. His hot breath rushed across the side of my face. It was almost enough to distract me. "What's wrong, Rae?"

"Nothing," I mumbled.

"Please don't lie to me," he said softly.

A heavy weight settled on my chest. I wonder how *he* liked being lied to.

"I'm not the only liar in this car," I snapped in a hushed whisper.

Venn's eyebrows drew together. "Rae…"

I spoke so quietly that only he could hear. "I just thought…" I hated feeling this way.

"That we were going after your sister?" he finished for me. "We will. We are."

"Are we?" I whispered.

I didn't know why I said that. All I knew was that my hopes had been crushed once again. My chest tightened, and my face heated. All I wanted was to shift into raven form so that he couldn't see my expression.

"Hey, Sondra," Venn said. "If it's cool with you, Rae and I have some unfinished business to attend to—"

"Venn, no," I protested under my breath. It wasn't fair of me to ask him to do this. I could do this on my own. I didn't *want* to, but I could.

Venn lowered his voice again just for me. "I promised I'd help you find your sister after we rescued Sondra. I don't break my promises."

My chest suddenly seemed ten pounds lighter, but it still didn't seem right to accept his generous offer.

"Where are you going to go?" Sondra asked.

Venn bit his lower lip. "I'm not sure, but we have to start somewhere. Rae's looking for her sister, and we believe she might be at a place called Gregor Island. Have you heard of it?"

Sondra thought about it for a second, then shook her head. Of course she didn't know. Not even the Internet knew anything about Gregor Island. Maybe Maliya had lied to us.

Filthy vampires.

"We believe it's where the Soulless are hiding," Venn said.

Sondra's eyes widened, and Fiona's pointed ears perked up. Even in her fox form, I could see the frown on her face. She looked terrified for us.

"You know you can't go," Teagan protested.

"We already talked about this, Tea," Venn replied. "Rae's stubborn, and she's going after her sister with or without us. I'm not letting her go alone."

Swoon.

"You know what you're getting into, don't you?" Sondra asked, as if in warning.

"Yes," I answered automatically. And it was worth it. For Jenna. I turned to Venn. "But you don't have to come with me. I don't want you to get hurt."

Who was I kidding? I definitely wanted him to come with me. But it was true that I didn't want to see him hurt.

Venn brushed a piece of hair behind my ear. "That's exactly why I'm going with you, Rae."

Out of the corner of my eye, I swore I saw Teagan roll her eyes from the front seat. Because she *totally* wasn't all over Ryland all the time.

"You're sure?" Sondra asked Venn. "I mean, if you—"

"I'm sure," he cut her off. "You need to get the Artifact, and we need to find Jenna."

I shot Venn a small smile.

"How are you going to get around?" Sondra asked.

"We'll rent a car," Venn decided.

Sondra raised an eyebrow. "And you'll stay in touch?"

Venn nodded. "Every step of the way."

Sondra pursed her lips—like she wasn't ready to tell Venn goodbye but knew she couldn't talk him out of this. "I don't want you going by yourself."

"But we—" Venn started.

Sondra cut him off. "There may be something else we can do."

My curiosity piqued.

"We'll split up for a few hours," Sondra said. "You can look for information on Rae's sister while we gather supplies. We'll meet up when we're both finished."

"I'm guessing you know where we should start?" Venn replied.

"I know a witch named Clarita who might have some information on the Soulless," Sondra told him. "Luckily for you, she's on the way."

3

The tension in the air was palpable the moment Venn and I stepped into the elevator at Clarita's condo. Venn pressed a button, and the doors slid shut, trapping us alone inside. We stood side-by-side facing the door, neither of us daring to steal a glance at the other.

Venn was close enough that I could smell his familiar scent. It made my insides go haywire. Every muscle in my body told me to turn to him and jump into his arms, to press my body against his and tangle my fingers in his hair. I wanted him to kiss me back like he meant it, to touch me in places I'd never been touched before. The surface of my skin heated just thinking about it. It was crazy what being alone with a guy for barely a second could do to your basic instincts.

Except Venn wasn't just any guy. He was *the* guy, the one I could picture giving everything to and spending the rest of my life with.

I'm going to have his shifter babies someday.

What the hell? Where did that come from? Behave, brain.

Venn broke the silence. "Are we ever going to talk about it?"

I glanced to him and tucked a loose strand of hair behind my ear. I willed myself not to blush, but my pale skin betrayed me. "Talk about what?"

Venn must've thought I was stupid, because the look in his eyes gave everything away. Couldn't we just make out and let the moment speak for itself?

"*You* know," he said with a teasing smile. "Don't you feel the crazy connection between us?"

Of course I did, but I wasn't about to admit it out loud. Except, with Venn, I almost *wanted* to talk about it. It was weird. I didn't like sharing my feelings with anyone, but there was something about Venn—about his whole family—that made me want to open up.

Venn inched closer to me until his chest was only an inch away from mine. If I breathed too hard, my boobs were going to touch him. Not that that'd be a bad thing...

There was plenty of space in the elevator for both of us, but in that moment, it felt as if the walls were shrinking in on us—and not in a claustrophobic I-need-to-get-out-of-here kind of way. More in a way that made me feel secure and safe, and freakishly hot. Why was my skin burning up?

"I think you know I feel it, too," I whispered.

What the heck? I wasn't supposed to say things like that out loud. But something about it felt *good*. It felt *right*. Nothing had felt right in years, so speaking the truth to someone I trusted was a relief.

Venn reached up to brush my hair from my eyes. His touch sent an electric tingle across my cheek. I dropped my gaze, hoping he couldn't tell that he totally took my breath away. I killed vampires for fun. I wasn't supposed to be brought to my knees by the simple touch of a drop-dead gorgeous guy.

Don't kid yourself. You'll be dropping to your knees eventually.

I bit down on my lip to keep from smiling. *Get your mind out of the gutter, Rachel.*

"What should we do about it?" Venn whispered. His hot breath rushed across my face.

I inched backward. I wasn't sure why, considering all I wanted to do was close that small gap between us. Venn followed until my back was pressed up against the wall. My lower back dug into the metal rail that lined the perimeter of the elevator.

I suddenly realized what I was doing. I *wanted* him to advance on me, because it meant he wanted me. By the look in his eyes, he wanted me as much as—if not more than—I wanted him. A shot of adrenaline raced through my veins, and my heart slammed against my rib cage as I waited for Venn to make the next move.

He wrapped his arms around the rail on both sides of me, trapping me in. I made no effort to escape, though. This position was hot as hell. I'd stay trapped between his arms as long as he liked, if the fool would just kiss me already.

The elevator *dinged,* pulling me out of my trance. Venn jumped and turned toward the doors as they slid open. Reality came crashing down on me, reminding me why we were here.

Damn it. We had to get serious now.

Venn looked as disappointed as I felt.

"We'll pick this up later?" I suggested.

"Yeah," he said with a shy nod. "Right where we left off."

Good, I thought in relief. I had something to look forward to.

My heart slowed as we stepped out of the elevator on the

twelfth floor of Clarita's building. The long hall was lit with soft lighting, and the doors were spaced far apart. The spotless gray patterned carpet made the apartment building look like a luxury hotel.

When I heard the word *witch*, I pictured cauldrons and pointed hats, but I'd come to learn that they were as diverse as anyone. Some witches, like Genevieve, preferred the cobwebs-in-the-corner Halloween theme. Others, like Clarita White, opted for modern luxuries. Judging by the condominium she lived in, she hadn't let her powers go to waste.

We reached the end of the hall and stopped in front of a door marked *1212*. I took a breath and knocked.

A woman poked her head into the hallway. All I could see was her shoulder-length black hair with thick bangs that brushed the top of her cat-rimmed glasses. She glanced between Venn and me.

"You're the ones Sondra called about?" she asked before either of us had a chance to speak.

"Yes," Venn answered. "May we come in?"

Clarita swung the door open, and I finally got a good look at her. She was at least three inches shorter than me with a curvy figure that filled out the dark purple dress she wore. Long earrings with rainbow-colored feathers attached dangled from her ears. Gorgeous blue beads hung from her neck, and she wore all different kinds of rings on each of her fingers.

She shot us a friendly smile. Clarita had a vibrant glow about her that I instantly connected with. She gave off serious *cool aunt* vibes, like she was the kind of person you could say anything to and get the best advice in return.

"Can I get you anything?" Clarita asked as we stepped inside. "Perhaps tea or water?"

"Water's fine," I answered.

Clarita gestured for us to sit while she closed the door behind us and headed to the kitchen. Her condo walls were white, but the decor was accented in every color of the rainbow. Pink, green, and blue throw pillows filled the couch and matched the bright floral pattern of her area rug. A coffee table with a stack of books on it sat in the center of the room, and a large-screen TV hung on the wall opposite the couch. Glass doors with long drapes beside them led out onto a balcony, and potted plants dotted the room. The condo wasn't huge—Clarita only seemed to have as much as she needed—but it was nice enough that I was sure it cost more to live here than what I made in a month.

I sank into the couch next to Venn. The cushions were so soft I could've fallen asleep right then and there.

"Here you go." Clarita returned and handed us each a bottled water. It was cold in my hand and refreshing when I took a sip.

"What do you do for work?" I couldn't help but let my curiosity get to me.

Clarita sat in the plush armchair across from us. "I own a boutique shop not far from here. It's been my dream since I was a kid."

"You don't work in magic?" Venn asked. He sounded surprised, like every other witch he'd met used their magic for profit.

"I used to," Clarita said as she adjusted her glasses. "Now I only work with a select few clients. What is it that I can help you with?"

Venn and I exchanged a glance. This wasn't the type of conversation you approached lightly.

Venn leaned forward and rested his elbows on his knees.

He spoke slowly. "Sondra said you might know something about the Soulless."

Clarita's right eyebrow twitched slightly, but apart from that, she didn't let her thoughts show. She took a long, deep breath and then let it out in a sigh. "I'm afraid I can't tell you much."

My body went so numb that my water bottle slipped out of my fingers and landed on the cushion beside me.

"It's true that I've had an interest in the Soulless for many years," Clarita said. "I, along with many other witches, am quite interested in learning what happened to them. We know how they came to be, but we don't know where they disappeared to when they went silent two years ago. Some suspect they're planning something big and that they'll be returning in full force soon."

"What do *you* think?" Venn asked.

Clarita straightened in her chair. "I haven't reached a clear conclusion yet. I've been trying to track them down for years, hoping that if we could infiltrate their nest, we might be able to figure out what they're planning. So far, I've only come up with guesses. Tracking spells, unfortunately, can be quite tricky without a starting point."

"Like how you need something that belongs to a person to track them?" I asked, remembering how we'd used Cowen's watch to track him.

"Exactly," Clarita confirmed. "But in this case, since we're looking for a hidden location, it starts with information. Unfortunately, we don't have enough of it."

"Information like what?" I asked slowly, wondering if what Venn and I learned from Maliya was enough.

"A general location would be a good start," Clarita said. "We know the Soulless are somewhere in the States, but reports are pretty widespread. We suspect their nest is located in the Midwest, but each time I perform the spell to narrow the location, I hit a block. It's like an ocean I can't cross."

Almost literally.

"That's because it is," I said in a rush.

She tilted her head in question.

"We believe the Soulless are hiding on an island somewhere in the Great Lakes," I elaborated. "But the lakes are so big that we don't know where to go from there. We were hoping you could help us figure it out."

Clarita pressed her lips together and shook her head. "We've tried the Great Lakes region, and nothing has ever come up."

I looked to Venn, my eyes widening. "Maliya lied to us."

Venn's lips tightened. "I don't know… I thought I could read her pretty well, and I believed she was telling the truth." He looked back to Clarita. "The island would've been cloaked by magic up until eight years ago, when Valkas escaped. It could still be cloaked."

Clarita stared into the distance in thought. "So Valkas is still in the same location he was imprisoned?"

Venn nodded.

"Mm…" Clarita mused. "Then why haven't *you* found him yet?"

"What do you mean?" I asked.

"You are a witch, aren't you?" Clarita responded.

I nodded, my heart rate spiking. "How could you tell?"

She smiled that soft, friendly smile of hers. "I'm a high witch. I can sense the magic around me, and you, sweetheart, radiate it. Perhaps I'm mistaken, but I sense you have a strong connection with the Soulless."

I looked to Venn, as if he might be able to explain what she meant by that. "I guess so. I mean, they kidnapped my sister, so I'm pretty motivated to find them and get her back."

"No." Clarita shook her head. "I meant a connection that spans many lifetimes."

Clarita stood and crossed around the mahogany coffee table to stand in front of me. She sat on the table casually, as if it were a chair, and held out an inviting hand. I hesitated.

"It's okay," she encouraged.

I glanced to Venn. He seemed relaxed enough, and I trusted his judgement, so I offered her my palm.

Clarita lifted her glasses and pulled my palm close to her face. She eyed it intensely, as though trying to burn a hole through it with laser vision. After studying my palm for what felt like a full minute, she closed her eyes and inhaled a deep breath. Finally, she opened them and dropped my palm.

Clarita readjusted her glasses. "It's very clear that your past lives are deeply rooted in history. I suspect you were among one of the witches to imprison Valkas."

I drew in a sharp breath. She was wrong. No way did my past lives involve powerful magic like that.

"I suppose you don't remember that yet, do you?" Clarita asked.

I shook my head. I couldn't seem to form any words in that moment. Clarita spoke so casually, like it wasn't a huge revelation. She had to be lying to me.

"You're much stronger than you think you are," Clarita said. "You have yet to realize your full potential in this life."

"That's what I told her," Venn chimed in.

I sat there dumbstruck. I was still trying to wrap my head around this whole past lives thing, let alone entertain the possibility that I'd been there to imprison the original vampire. It was clear I wasn't quite the low witch I'd always thought I was, but I wasn't powerful, either. Clarita was insane.

Clarita stood and crossed over to a cupboard set into the wall. She began shuffling through it while she spoke. "Is there anything else you can tell me about the location of the Soulless?"

"Yes," Venn answered confidently. "We were told the Soulless are residing in a place called Gregor Island."

Clarita's eyes lit up as she turned from the cupboards. She held a large roll of paper in one hand and a black marker in the other. She bounced on her toes in excitement. "That's excellent! You know the name! If it's true, pinpointing the location should be simple."

My heart soared in excitement. *One step closer.*

Clarita lowered herself to her knees and swept the books off the coffee table, as if they were unimportant. She unrolled the paper in her hand to reveal a large laminated map of the United States. I leaned forward to get a better look.

"Can you get the drapes?" Clarita asked.

Venn quickly rose to his feet and rounded the couch. He pulled the drapes shut, and the room was instantly blanketed in darkness. Only a small amount of light peeked through the edges of the curtain.

"The dark helps me concentrate," Clarita said to no one in particular. "Let's get started."

In the darkness, I could only see silhouettes. Clarita reached up and slipped a set of beads off of her neck. She held them straight out and dangled them above the map.

The cushion beside me sank in as Venn returned to his spot. I barely noticed him, though. Clarita had stolen my attention.

She closed her eyes and began muttering unfamiliar words

under her breath. To my amazement, the beads in her hand began to sway, though Clarita hadn't moved an inch. The room sizzled with energy that only grew with each passing second. I could feel it brush across my skin, raising the hairs on my arms.

The beads swirled clockwise and increased their speed without expanding the small imaginary circle they were outlining. Clarita's eyes remained closed, and she continued to mutter words I didn't understand. Her hand opened, but the beads remained suspended in mid-air.

My heart hammered as I witnessed the magic unfold before my eyes. I'd seen spells performed before, but this was different. The beads seemed to have a mind of their own and moved as if gravity didn't matter. It was mesmerizing, and honestly a little freaky. This went far beyond the laws of physics.

The beads slowly descended through the air, as if they were connected to a wire. They stopped when the lowest bead touched the map, though they continued to hang there, circling a small area of blue in the northernmost part of Lake Michigan.

My breath ceased. Had we found it?

Clarita's eyes snapped open. Almost instantly, the beads fell into a heap on top of the map. She brushed them aside and popped the cap off her marker. She quickly drew an X right where the beads had been hovering and then looked to us in alarm.

"You must go." She spoke so fast that the words all jumbled together.

Clarita jumped to her feet while she rolled up the map. Venn and I both shot up from the couch at once. Tension suddenly overtook my entire body.

"What's wrong?" I demanded.

"Here, take this." Clarita shoved the map into my hands. "But don't use it yet."

I opened my mouth to demand an explanation of what was going on, but she was already ushering us to the door.

"Hold on," Venn insisted. "What—?"

"Go to your family," Clarita interrupted. "They need you."

"What do you mean?" I demanded. My body broke out in a sweat. Was Venn's family in danger? "What's happening?"

Clarita swung the front door open. "I cannot tell specifics, only that you need to return to them now."

Venn opened his mouth to say more, but Clarita grabbed a set of keys from the small table in her entryway and shoved them in his hands.

"Take my car," she insisted. "The parking garage is down the hall and to the left."

Venn and I both seemed to realize at the same moment how serious Clarita was. It didn't matter what she knew or how she knew it. It was clear there wasn't time for explanations.

Venn shot me one glance of horror and then grabbed my hand.

"Wait!" Clarita called before we made it too far.

I whirled around to face her, my heart hammering.

She stood in her doorway. "I mean it about the map, Rae. If you use it before helping your family with their current quest, you and your sister have no hope of making it off Gregor Island alive."

My blood ran cold.

"Now go," Clarita said in a rush. "Your family can no longer wait."

4

———

Heavy raindrops pounded against the windshield of Clarita's car, obscuring our view of the street in front of us. The wipers swiped as fast as they could, but it wasn't enough. People rushed off the streets to escape the downpour, and the traffic in front of us slowed.

"Venn—what if—what do you think—?" I couldn't get the words out as the possibilities raced through my mind. "There has to be a faster way."

Venn spun around in his seat, glancing up and down the street. His eyebrows were tight, but he didn't voice his worry like I had. In front of us, a vehicle pulled into traffic from where it had been parked on the curb.

"Hang on," Venn said in a rush. He pulled the wheel to the right and whipped into the parking spot.

He rushed out into the rain, and I quickly followed behind him. I was drenched in under a second, but I didn't care. All I cared about was making sure Venn's family was all right.

"How far?" I shouted.

Venn grabbed my hand and began sprinting down the sidewalk. "Not far!" he called back.

The crosswalk up ahead signaled *walk* as soon as we approached it, and we raced across the street. We hurried past shop after shop and weaved past groups of people. No one took notice to us, as we simply looked like a couple who had forgotten their umbrellas.

Venn turned right at the end of the block. The sidewalk was nearly empty here, since most people had already escaped the rain. We passed by a coffee shop, and then a café, before spotting a sign that read *Amalia's*.

"Venn, your car!" I pointed to the black car parked further down the street. It should've brought me comfort knowing we'd found Venn's family, but it only made my anxiety flare. What if we were too late?

Venn whipped open the door to Amalia's, and I rushed inside. I didn't know what I expected to find, but I was shocked by the quiet atmosphere. Neatly stocked shelves filled with books and herbs lined the outer walls of the small shop. Candles, crystals, essential oils, and various other items filled the tables in the middle of the room. The shop was bathed in natural wood tones and accented in earthy colors.

There were two women to our right who were soaking wet and looked as if they'd only entered the shop to get out of the rain. Another lady browsed the shelves toward the back of the store.

A blonde who looked around Sondra's age glanced up at us from behind the checkout desk. Venn rushed over to her.

"Can I help you?" she asked. There was a hint of recognition in her eye when she looked at Venn.

"Yes," Venn said breathlessly. "Sondra. Have you seen her?"

The blonde smiled. "Oh, that's where I know you from. I was trying to figure it out."

"This is urgent," Venn pressed.

The woman's eyes grew wide. "I'm sorry. I haven't seen her since—"

Venn cursed under his breath and whirled around before she could finish her sentence. I rushed behind him back outside into the pouring rain. Venn raced down the sidewalk.

"You don't think...?" I started, but I couldn't finish my sentence.

"I don't know what I think—" Venn's words died on his tongue as a scream cut through the air. He skidded to a halt once we reached the end of the block.

I stopped behind him. Down the next street, shadows moved through the thick rain. A deep roar met my ears, and a creature as big as a bear rose to its hind legs. *Ryland.* Three other female figures moved through the rain—Fiona, Teagan, and Sondra. At least four other guys retaliated against them.

The breath left my chest. We'd found Venn's family, and it wasn't good. At all.

Venn sprinted forward and shifted into a wolf mid-stride. I raced behind him. Venn slammed into the nearest vamp, who had Fiona by the back of the neck. He stumbled backward and released her. The first thought that went through my mind was to ignite a fire under his feet and watch him burn, but I knew even my magical fire wouldn't burn in this type of downpour. My gaze flickered upward, cursing the skies.

And that's when I saw the tiger. One story up on a metal fire escape, a massive orange cat peeked over the railing, watching Ryland's every move. He adjusted his legs, calibrating for attack.

Damn it. We weren't just dealing with vampires here. We were facing shifters, and this one might actually stand a chance against Ryland.

I didn't think about what I was doing. I just acted. My body shrank to the size of a raven, and I spread my wings. Rain hammered down on my feathers, and it took every ounce of strength I had to push against it and fly through the sky. A gust of wind caught my wings and hurled me off course. I quickly corrected my flight and continued on my intended path.

To my horror, the tiger shifter was already making the leap. I dove as fast as I could toward him. Disgust twisted in my gut as I felt my talons slice deeply across the skin between his eyes. A roar filled the street as the tiger fell through the air.

I landed on the closest fire escape and held tightly to the metal. The tiger landed on Ryland's back, but I could see that the roar had alerted him. Ryland spun around, and his jaws clamped upon the tiger's paw.

Lightning cracked through the street. But it hadn't come from the sky. I could've sworn it had come straight from Sondra's hands, blasting back one of the men. As fast as it was there, it was gone. I only paused a moment to take in the scene before I was swooping down to the street again. I glanced around frantically, hoping to find something to use as a weapon. I found nothing. I would have to fight with what I had: my talons and beak.

Before I had a chance to reach the fight, the man Sondra had blasted backward hopped to his feet. Freaking vampires and their immortality. Even through the downpour, I could see the fury in his eyes as he fixed them on Sondra.

I flew forward and dug my talons into the back of his neck. He cried out in pain and whirled around to fling me off of him. My small body whipped through the air and slammed against the side of the brick building. I sank to the ground and gasped for breath.

When I glanced up, Lightning Guy was sauntering toward me. Terror filled my chest when I realized his eyes weren't silver. They were blue. Which meant he wasn't a vampire. To survive the kind of shock Sondra had just given him, he must've been—

Lightning Guy raised his palms and muttered an incantation under his breath. I spread my wings, but I already knew I wasn't going to make it out of the way in time. A blast of dark green energy erupted out of his palms.

I flinched, but before I felt the blast hit me, a dark shadow crossed in front of me. I opened my eyes to see Venn writhing on the sidewalk in pain. Slowly, his arms and legs lengthened as his body shifted back into human form. He stared straight up into the sky while the rain pounded down on him. His body convulsed uncontrollably.

The blood drained from my face as I quickly shifted back into human form and knelt beside him.

"Venn, no!" I cried, leaning over him.

His gaze traveled straight through me.

I shot to my feet and narrowed my gaze at Lightning Guy. "Fuck you!" I screamed.

He only laughed as he gazed down at Venn in satisfaction.

"*Ardeat ignis,*" I mumbled under my breath.

The hem of Lightning Guy's jeans caught on fire. It burned, despite the dampness of the fabric, but the rain had put it out before he even noticed.

Lightning cracked across the street again, pulling the guy's attention away from us. His face fell when he realized only he and the tiger shifter remained. The tiger shifter ran as fast as he could on three feet toward Lightning Guy. Ryland sprinted behind him, limping on his bad leg, and Lighting Guy took off running alongside his tiger friend.

I didn't watch to see how far Ryland chased them down the street. Instead, I fell hopelessly to my knees beside Venn. Boils had erupted across his face, marring his handsome features.

"Stay with me, Venn." I placed my hands on his shoulders, but he only shook more violently under my touch. I ran my fingers down his arm and squeezed his hand tightly. It was beginning to swell.

I was aware of several other figures kneeling down beside us, but I didn't quite register them until a voice spoke.

"We have to get him inside. Now." I recognized the voice as the blonde from inside Amalia's. She must've followed us outside.

Sondra stood beside the blonde and mumbled something under her breath. To my surprise, Venn's body elevated off the pavement, as if being carried on an invisible stretcher. My sobs ceased instantly, and I rose beside him. Venn continued to shake and stare lifelessly up at the sky.

"Is he going to be okay?" Fiona asked.

Sondra turned her eyes away and didn't answer. That couldn't be a good sign.

"He'll be okay," Teagan said softly, wrapping an arm around Fiona. "He has to be."

"This way," the blonde said in a rush, gesturing for us to follow her.

She led us down an alley, past various doors and dumpsters. We followed her inside a door that I could only presume led to the back of Amalia's. She glanced up and down the alleyway. Ryland rushed forward in human form and entered the hallway we stood in.

"They got away," he said through heavy breaths.

The blonde shut the door and whirled around. She rushed past each of us in the narrow hall. "You're safe here. My shop is heavily guarded with protection spells." She flung open another door. "In here."

"Oh my God," Ryland whispered, his eyes fixed on Venn.

Fiona responded, but I was too overwhelmed to hear what exactly she'd said.

Sondra guided Venn into a small room no bigger than my studio apartment. There was a small kitchenette against one corner and a big burgundy couch against another. The break room had similar decor as the main shop. I figured the soft lighting and earthy tones were meant to be relaxing, but I couldn't relax right then.

Sondra lowered Venn onto the couch, but he continued to convulse. I froze near the door and swallowed my emotions, pushing them down far into the pit of my stomach. My guts felt like rocks. I wanted to rush over to Venn, to cast a healing spell over him, but I knew my healing abilities wouldn't help.

I couldn't even combat the effects of vampire venom. I wasn't going to reverse another witch's spell.

"What do you have, Amalia?" Sondra asked.

"I might have something," the blonde responded, "but it's going to take three of us. We could call Clarita—"

"There's no time," Sondra insisted. "This curse will take over his body in minutes. Rae, get over here. We have to act now."

"Rae!" Sondra repeated my name while Amalia hurried out of the room. I suddenly snapped to attention.

"They need three witches to run the spell," Fiona told me. "You can do it, Rae. You're good at healing."

"Regular injuries," I emphasized. "Not supernatural ones."

"Well, you're going to have to do your best." Teagan grabbed my shoulders and forced me forward until I was standing right beside Venn.

I turned my face away. I didn't want to remember him like that, the way he stared straight through me. It was terrifying.

"Why can't you heal him yourself?" I asked Sondra. "You're a high witch."

"Because," Amalia answered as she returned to the break room. She held a stack of glass vials in her arms and dumped them on the table nearby. "Breaking another witch's spell is almost impossible. Can you grab me a bowl from that cupboard?"

Amalia pointed above the kitchenette, and Fiona quickly crossed the room and retrieved a large mixing bowl. Amalia began pouring contents of the vials together in various amounts.

"In most cases, only the witch who cast the spell can break it," Amalia explained, "but this spell is weak enough that we might be able to save him."

I dared to steal a glance at Venn. Weak spell my ass. His eyes were swollen shut, and I was pretty sure he was on the brink of losing his breath.

"If you don't want your friend to die, I need your help," Amalia insisted.

She held out two vials, each full of a clear liquid. Sondra stepped forward and took one. Amalia stretched her arm out further, encouraging me to take the other.

I cleared my throat, willing my voice to stay strong. "What do I have to do?"

"Calm down, Rae," Sondra said in a soothing voice.

I couldn't understand how she remained calm at a time like this—or how she expected me to.

"Magic works best without anxiety or tension," Sondra said, as if she were coaching me. "Venn has a better chance of survival if you can let all that negative energy go."

If she thought that was a comforting way to put it, she was way off the mark. But the fact was, I was wasting time standing there. I needed to do exactly what I was told, for Venn's sake. Emotions be damned. I'd control them, not let them control me.

I snatched the vial out of Amalia's hand. Behind me, Fiona and Teagan stood beside Venn and did their best to comfort him. Ryland stuck his hands in his pockets near the door, looking shook. It seemed like he wanted to help but didn't know what to do.

"We'll save him," Sondra whispered reassuringly beside me.

I forced myself to believe her.

"When we're all ready, I want you to repeat these words with me while we all pour our oils together into the bowl, okay?" Amalia said in a serious tone. "*Sana carissimi nahil pati.*"

I repeated the words aloud, testing them on my tongue.

"Not until you're ready, though," Amalia warned.

We were running out of time. If I wasn't ready to perform magic in the next five seconds, I might lose Venn.

I didn't let myself think about that. Instead, I closed my eyes and pictured his sweet face, letting the warmth of his smile wash over me. Memories of the morning after I met him flickered through my mind, how he'd stayed in my apartment to clean my wound while I was passed out and had made sure I was all right. I recalled our friendly banter, how I teased that the first thing he'd tell his family about me was that I let him strip my pants off on our first meeting. I cracked a smile. I wasn't sure he'd actually told anyone that.

Venn better live, because he still needs to take my pants off and get in them this time.

I let out a deep breath, letting the tension in my shoulders melt away with it. Deep down, I was still a nervous wreck, but this was the best I could do.

"Ready?" Sondra asked, eyeing me with concern.

"Ready," I stated.

Amalia lifted her vial and began the incantation. Sondra and I joined in, repeating it over and over again until our vials were completely empty. The liquid mixture in the bowl swirled on its own accord, transforming into pink, then purple, before finally settling on dark blue. Amalia dipped her fingers into the potion. It dripped from her hand in a thick paste.

"Each of us will take about this much and spread it across his skin," she explained. "The rest he will have to drink."

I didn't ask how we were going to get the paste down his throat. Fiona and Teagan quickly stepped aside as Amalia, Sondra, and I approached.

"Each of you take a hand, and keep repeating the incantation," Amalia instructed as she wiped the blue substance across Venn's inflamed face.

I focused my attention on his fingers, which had swollen to the size of sausages. I rubbed a glob across his dark skin. It spread evenly and soaked into it like lotion.

Venn coughed violently, causing my anxiety to spring back to the surface. Amalia pulled the bowl away from his mouth. Blue goop the consistency of yogurt ran down his lips.

"He's choking!" I cried.

Sondra grabbed my wrist before I could reach his head and help him. "Hang on. It's working."

Just as she said it, Venn's coughing ceased. The thick potion slid down his throat, and the convulsions stopped.

"He's going to be okay?" I asked, glancing between Sondra and Amalia.

Amalia placed the bowl back up to Venn's lips and forced more of the potion into his mouth. "It'll take a couple of hours before we know for sure. We've done all we can."

To be honest, I didn't feel like I'd done anything. Boils still covered his face, and his eyes were still swollen shut. At best, we slowed down the curse's progress, but I wasn't sure we'd reversed the effects.

"We just need to give him time to recover now," Sondra

said somberly as she stepped away from Venn. "He's a fighter. He'll be all right."

I wanted to believe her. I had to.

I sank to the floor next to the couch and leaned my head against one of the cushions. I held on to Venn's hand and stroked his skin, praying to every god I'd ever heard of that he would survive.

At some point, I closed my eyes, and my consciousness drifted away.

I gazed down at my hands. I knew they were mine because they were attached to my body, but they didn't look like my hands. The fingers were longer and the nails the wrong shape, but the abnormalities didn't seem to register in the moment.

"I need your hand," I instructed in a voice that sounded familiar, as if I'd been hearing it my whole life. But at the same time, it was like I'd never heard it before. I spoke with a thick British accent. It felt perfectly natural, like I'd been born with it.

A hand came into view, though I didn't look up to see who the hand belonged to. Somehow, I knew it was a man, despite the smooth skin and neat fingernails. I grabbed on to his wrist and held his hand over a wooden bowl.

"This is going to hurt," I warned him.

"I know," the man replied in an equally thick accent. "I'm prepared."

My heart hammered as I picked up a dagger sitting on the table beside my bowl. Somehow, I knew it was the man's dagger. I gazed down at the embellishments on the handle, knowing I'd never be able to afford something like this on my own.

I placed the blade to his palm. My hands shook, and I hesitated.

"Do as you're told, witch," the man snarled. He said the word witch *like it was poison on his tongue.*

I swallowed hard and then dragged the blade across his skin, cutting deeper than I needed to. I wanted the man to hurt. I wanted him to suffer. Every instinct told me that he deserved it.

Blood poured out of the wound, filling the bowl with a crimson liquid. The man didn't make a sound, as if he was immune to the pain.

"I hope this is what you truly want," I said.

"It is," the man growled. "I will not let the fate of man claim me."

I jerked awake. The details of my dream began to slip away the moment my eyes opened. I mentally clamored to hold on to the memory, though I wasn't sure why I bothered. It was only a dream.

I blinked, trying to remember where I was. I stared up at a white ceiling bathed in soft lighting. The surface beneath me was hard and uncomfortable.

"Have you heard of it?" a female voice asked from across the room.

I pushed myself up. I'd been lying on the floor in Amalia's break room beside the couch. Venn lay there with his eyes closed, his chest rising and falling slowly. The boils on his face had completely disappeared, though there was still swelling around his eyes. His hands had slimmed and looked like his again. I ran my fingers across the soft skin on his cheek. It felt like he was running a fever of a hundred degrees.

"Rae."

Fiona's voice caught my attention. I jerked away from

Venn as if I'd been caught doing something wrong. I looked up to see everyone else seated at the break table.

I rubbed the sleep from my eyes. "Why didn't anyone wake me up?"

Ryland shrugged. "You looked peaceful. Plus, Tea said you'd probably stab my eye out if I woke you."

I couldn't argue with that.

"What's going on?" I asked.

"Why don't you come sit by us?" Sondra suggested, gesturing to the empty chair beside them.

I glanced between it and Venn. I didn't want to leave his side.

"Venn could use some space," Amalia said. "He needs to heal."

No way, bitch, was my first reaction. I almost let it slip out, too.

"I'm fine here, thanks," I said instead. "Can someone fill me in on what happened? Who were those guys?"

"They were some of Matias's men," Sondra answered. "I recognized one of the guys from his security team. He must've sent them to follow us to make sure we weren't trying to double-cross him or something. We noticed them following and confronted them."

I nodded in understanding.

"Amalia was just going to tell us what she knows about the Artifact." Fiona sounded excited.

I sat with my back to the couch and draped Venn's limp arm across my chest. My fingers laced in his. I placed a light kiss on the back of his hand while I listened.

"It sounds like the artifact you're describing is the *Sapiens noctua,* otherwise known as The Wise Owl," Amalia said. "I remember my great aunt saying something about it before she passed. She was the only other witch in my family."

Sondra leaned forward. "What'd she say about it?"

Amalia shrugged. "Just that it was very old. It was created centuries ago by a group of witches who wanted to block another witch's powers, one who was using magic for all the wrong reasons. I don't think it was ever intended to be used on a mass scale, only for the greater good."

"Did your aunt ever say what the object actually was?" Teagan asked.

Amalia shook her head.

Ryland shifted in his chair. "Did she mention where to find it or how to destroy it?"

"No," Amalia answered in a regretful tone. "All I know is that when magic returned, my aunt became very interested in it, to the point where her kids thought she'd gone completely off her rocker. She became very involved in the magical community and taught me most of what I know, though her magic was a lot more advanced than mine. I think she got a lot of her information from her past lives. I have yet to remember anything from mine."

"You believe in reincarnation?" I asked. "And Synchrony?"

How did everyone I meet just know this stuff when the rest of the world still thought we were in the middle of the apocalypse?

"Yes," Amalia replied, "but only because my aunt told me. Most witches can perform magic but don't actually know how it works."

It sounded like my boss, Devin.

"So, your aunt remembered The Wise Owl?" Fiona guessed.

"No, actually, she read about it in a book," Amalia said. "A few years ago, my aunt got her hands on a book that explained a lot of the truth about magic and had chapters on known magical artifacts and their history. If you want to learn more about The Wise Owl, I think your best bet is finding that book."

"You don't know where it is?" Sondra asked.

Amalia's lips tightened. "No, unfortunately. My aunt left it to me, but her kids ignored her wishes and sold it instead."

"You never tried to track it down?" Sondra asked.

"Of course I did!" Amalia sounded slightly offended. "But it's loaded with protection charms."

"Is there anything else you can tell us about the book?" Teagan asked.

Amalia shook her head. "All I remember is that it was a good six inches thick with a leather binding. It had images of the sun, moon, and stars on the front cover. That's all I can tell you."

Venn stirred next to me. I immediately whirled around and knelt beside him. Everyone else in the room stilled.

"Venn, talk to me." I stroked my fingers through his curls.

He grunted. It sounded like he was trying to speak, but I couldn't tell what he was saying.

"What?" I demanded. "Venn..."

"Genevieve," he managed to croak out.

Excuse me? It's Rachel, your girlfriend.

"No, Venn. It's me. Rae. You're going to be okay." I was practically on the verge of tears just from hearing his voice.

Venn's eyes opened into slits. "No, the book. Genevieve."

Fiona drew in a sharp breath beside me. I hadn't even realized she'd crossed the room. "Venn's right. I remember a book like that at Genevieve's."

Sondra stood beside Fiona and looked down at Venn,

concern for him etched in her eyes. "I think you might be right. I didn't pay any attention to it before, but…"

Ryland sighed. "Well, we can kiss that big paycheck goodbye."

I looked at him still seated beside Amalia and Teagan across the room. "What do you mean?"

Teagan crossed her arms and leaned back in her seat. "We have a bit of debt with Genevieve."

Ryland scoffed. "A bit."

"And she's not going to help us without payment," Teagan said.

"She helped us before," I pointed out.

"That's because I wasn't there," Sondra said. "My old mentor… isn't fond of me."

My eyes nearly bulged out of my skull. I couldn't imagine a pure-hearted witch like Sondra working with someone dark like Genevieve.

Teagan stood from her chair. "When do we leave?"

Sondra glanced back to Venn, who had gone still again. I pressed my palm to his forehead. He was still burning up.

"We have to stay here overnight," Sondra said. "Venn's still healing."

"Tea and I will take the car," Ryland suggested.

"No," Sondra replied almost instantly. "I want us all to stick together. We'll get a hotel for the night and all rest up. We'll head to Genevieve's in the morning."

"You think she'll help us?" Fiona said softly.

Sondra hesitated. "God, I hope so."

6

Venn was hotter than cement on a summer day, and I meant that in a literal sense, though his body was smoking hot as well. I lay beside him on the queen-sized bed in our hotel room. Heat radiated off his skin like a furnace. He was running a fever hotter than any human should. But Venn wasn't exactly human.

"Are you going to give the guy space or what?" Ryland lay on the bed beside us, leaning his back against the headboard and flipping the channels on the TV.

"No," I answered automatically.

Fiona flung a pillow at Ryland while she made up the sofa bed for her and Sondra across the room. "Give her a break. It's not like you wouldn't be doing the same to Teagan if she'd been cursed."

"Whatever," Ryland said with an eye roll.

"Don't kid yourself, babe," Teagan teased from beside him. "You'd be all over me."

Ryland shot her a glare.

The door to our hotel room opened, and Sondra strode in carrying two pizza boxes and a bottle of citrus soda.

Ryland sat up straight. "Seriously, Sondra? You know I'll eat a whole pizza by myself."

She placed the boxes at the foot of his bed and shrugged. "I'd like to see you try."

A sly smile crossed Ryland's face. "Challenge accepted."

Teagan slapped his arm when he pulled a whole pizza box into his lap. "You can share."

"Fine," he said begrudgingly as he opened the box and offered her a piece.

Fiona and Sondra were already digging into the other box.

"Aren't you hungry, Rae?" Fiona asked after taking a bite.

I shifted uncomfortably on the bed. "No. I'm okay."

Sondra eyed me with concern. "When was the last time you ate?"

Honestly, I couldn't remember, but my stomach had twisted into enough knots that I didn't feel hungry.

"Please come and eat something, Rae." Sondra spoke softly, but there was a mother-bear tone to her words that told me she would force feed me if she had to, just so I wouldn't starve to death.

I sighed and rose from the bed. It broke my heart to leave Venn's side, even though I was only a few feet away from him. Fiona scooted over on the foot of the bed so I could sit beside her. I grabbed a piece of pepperoni pizza and took small bites. Even though I wasn't hungry, I couldn't deny that it was delicious. Everyone went silent while they ate and watched an old cartoon play across the TV.

Everyone except Sondra. She sat in the chair in the corner and kept her eyes locked on me.

Finally, I couldn't take it anymore. "Do I have something on my face?"

Sondra sat up straighter. "No. I was just trying to figure out where I know you from. I thought I recognized you when we first met, but I think I finally know where I've met you before."

I glanced to Fiona, who looked intrigued but didn't say anything.

"I'm pretty sure we've never met," I said, though I couldn't deny there was something familiar in her eyes, too. I figured she just had one of those faces.

"Not in this life," Sondra agreed.

It took me a moment to realize what she was saying. I initially wrote it off as one of those things people say, but then it hit me that she could very well be serious.

"You—you think you remember me? From a past life?" I asked. It seemed weird to talk about it so casually, but something about past lives just made sense.

Sondra nodded. "And I think I know who you were."

My curiosity suddenly piqued. I finished my last bite of pizza and wiped my fingers across my jeans. "Who was I?"

Sondra finished her pizza and leaned forward in her chair. "I believe you were Abigail Williams."

Fiona inhaled a sharp breath. Someone else—probably Ryland—hit *mute* on the remote.

Abigail Williams. Where have I heard that name before?

The memory suddenly clicked. She was one of the faces on the wall back at Venn's house—before it'd burnt down. Sondra had drawn her face, like all the others. Venn had said she'd remembered the faces, which made complete sense now that I knew Sondra could remember bits and pieces from her past lives.

I racked my brain, trying to remember what Venn had told me about Abigail. She was a witch, I remembered that. But which one?

"You were still *you*," Sondra explained, misinterpreting my silence. "Just a different version of yourself. It was the same soul."

"What do you mean?" I asked. "What's a soul, anyway?"

"Your soul is what makes you... you," Sondra said. "It houses your empathy, your thoughts, and your most important memories."

"What does a soul look like?" I was completely intrigued. "Like a spirit?"

"Your soul isn't really a physical *thing*, more of an abstract idea, but I suppose you could visualize it as a ball of energy," Sondra said with a shrug. "When you die, your soul continues to exist on a separate plane. A spirit is the soul of someone who is between death and reincarnation. They can roam the earth, observe, and communicate with psychics, but a soul needs a body to exist physically."

"What happens to a soul once their body dies?" I asked.

"Those who have unfinished business might stick around," Sondra said. "Others will live again in another body."

"How does that work?" I glanced between Fiona and Sondra. "Reincarnation, I mean."

Fiona was the one to answer. "Synchrony assigns souls to bodies based on whatever will bring balance."

"Where do souls come from?" I questioned for my own curiosity.

"Synchrony creates new souls as new life blossoms," Fiona explained. "But so far, no one knows how to destroy a soul. The most you can do is trap them with a spell. Only Synchrony itself can destroy souls."

"Actually destroy them?" I asked in shock.

"It's only a theory," Sondra clarified. "Some witches believe that Synchrony's balance tips in favor of goodness, of positive energy. So when a soul turns evil, it is destroyed to maintain that balance."

Sondra sounded skeptical.

"What do you believe?" I asked.

She took a long breath before answering. "Look around you. There's evil everywhere. Greed, abuse, hatred... I'm not sure that story isn't just a scare tactic..."

Silence settled over the room before Sondra spoke again. "It doesn't pay to worry about it. Just focus on bringing your own goodness into the world. Life is easier that way."

I sat there silently, absorbing all this information. It was strange how for the first time in my life, it felt like I was listening to the truth rather than just another bogus theory.

"So, I'm Abigail?" I asked slowly, testing out the concept.

"Mm..." Sondra mused. "It's a little more complicated than that. You *were* Abigail, but now you're Rae."

"But you just said my soul is the same from one life to the next," I pointed out.

"Yes, it's the same soul," Sondra agreed, "but a different person, if that makes sense."

It didn't. Not really.

"The person you are in this life is shaped by both your soul and your experiences," Sondra explained. "Your past life experiences have some effect on you, but it doesn't mean you'll be the exact same person."

"Okay," I said slowly. "I think I get it. So, Abigail... who was she exactly?"

"She's the witch who created shifters," Fiona reminded me.

"Right," I said in realization. "She was married to that

Charles guy, who fused his body with a wolf's so they could track vampires."

"Yep," Fiona said. "Which makes total sense, because—"

"Because souls are drawn to each other from one life to the next," Sondra finished for her.

"You mean soulmates." I smiled, amused.

"Yes," Sondra confirmed, "but it's not just souls connected by romance that are drawn to each other, though that is the strongest bond. It can also happen with friends or family members, like a mother and child."

Everything they said made so much sense. I felt a sense of peace wash over me now that I knew the truth.

Venn's voice cut through the brief silence.

I quickly hurried to his side and took his hand. "What is it, Venn?"

"Eyes… window… soul," he managed to force out.

I looked to Fiona, like she might be able to translate for me.

Venn cleared his throat. "Eyes are the windows to the soul."

"Eyes are the windows to the soul?" I repeated.

Venn nodded.

"What does he mean?" I asked Sondra.

Sondra stood and crossed to the foot of the bed. "He means it quite literally. If you're magical enough—or if you had a very strong connection with that particular person in a past life—you can recognize a person's soul through their eyes."

A memory of Venn's words flashed through my head. *There's something in her eyes...*

He'd said that to Ryland when he'd brought me home with him. He was trying to convince Ryland I could be trusted.

And *his* eyes… Venn's soft brown eyes… maybe it hadn't been lust that drew me to him to begin with.

"It's true," Venn croaked. "Sondra told me ages ago that I was Charles."

Shock riveted through me, though I don't know why I was surprised. It made a lot of sense after just hearing that I was Abigail, his wife.

"So, you were the first shifter?" I asked.

Venn nodded.

"Ironic that you were a wolf shifter back then and a wolf shifter now," I thought aloud.

"Not really," Sondra said.

I looked to her for explanation.

"Shifter genes are genetic," she explained, "but you could end up *any* type of shifter once that DNA is in your blood. I personally believe that you shift into whatever animal matches your personality."

"Huh." I'd never thought of it that way before.

Beside me, Venn finally peeled his eyes open. My heart swooned under his gaze.

"You're okay," I said breathlessly as a smile spread across his face.

He nodded, but it sounded like it pained him to speak. "When I met you, I saw something in your eyes, Rae. The way it felt when I first saw you… it was like we'd lived a whole life together."

My insides danced, and the rest of the room faded away. I understood now why I was so comfortable around him, why I didn't mind spilling my secrets.

"I think I know what you mean," I whispered.

"Ugh," Teagan gagged. "Get a room."

"If you don't like it, you can leave," Venn teased back.

His eyes returned to mine, then traveled down to my lips. Oh, God. He was going to kiss me now, right in front of his whole family. Not that I didn't want him to, but the look in his eyes told me I didn't exactly want his family to see what he had in mind.

"You're feeling better?" I felt his forehead, which was still hot but had cooled down several degrees.

"A little bit," Venn said with a forced smile.

I smirked. "Then I can tell you what an idiot you were?"

He faked offense, but it was quickly replaced with a smile.

"You shouldn't have run in front of me," I scolded.

"This is the thanks I get?" he teased. "Rae, I'd run in front of you a thousand more times to make sure you don't get hurt."

I swore my heart skipped a literal beat. "You don't have to do that, Venn. I'd just reincarnate anyway."

Sadness filled his eyes. "That doesn't matter. I still don't want to see you hurt. And I don't want to wait to spend another lifetime with you."

Fair enough.

Venn reached up and brushed a strand of hair behind my ear. Then, in what felt like slow motion, he lifted his head and pressed his lips softly to mine. Fireworks exploded in my chest. My head spun, and I could hardly breathe.

Cheers filled the other side of the room, reminding me that there were other people watching us. My cheeks flamed red, but I kept my head down so that only Venn would see it.

"Shut up, you two," Fiona snapped at Teagan and Ryland, who were *whooping* and hollering at our expense. She hopped up from the bed to pour herself some soda. "I think it's sweet."

A hint of a smile crossed Sondra's face. "We should all get to bed. Everyone needs sleep."

She crawled into the pull-out bed, and Fiona climbed in beside her. It suddenly occurred to me that the only spot left to sleep was next to Venn. I didn't just stop breathing this time. I literally died.

Well, not literally, but close to it, I swear. I got to spend all night snuggled up next to this amazing creature? Sign me up!

Venn realized the same thing, and a grin spread across his face. He placed a chaste kiss on my nose and then pulled the covers away so I could crawl beneath them with him. I was still in my jeans as usual, but that didn't seem to matter. All that mattered was Venn's warm body pressed against mine. His cinnamon scent filled my nose, and his breath rushed across the back of my neck. His arm wrapped across my chest, and his legs curved around mine, as if our bodies were made to fit together like puzzle pieces.

I held my breath so he couldn't hear my heavy breathing. My heart thumped against my rib cage, as if it were trying to escape. That, I couldn't help, even though I worried Venn could feel it through my skin. My stomach danced with butterflies, and my body became so alive that I didn't believe there was any way in hell I was falling asleep tonight.

Which I guess was fine by me. It'd give me plenty of time to enjoy Venn's soothing embrace and the warmth of his body pressed closely against mine.

I couldn't remember the last time I was this happy. Probably never. The only times that ever came close were when my family was still alive…

Reality came crashing down on me all in a single instant. In my world, happiness was forever short-lived. This peaceful feeling would be gone as soon as we went back to slaying vampires and searching for the Artifact.

Tonight, I was going to enjoy Venn's company while I could. Tomorrow, it was back to my cruel, harsh reality.

7

"I'll be damned." Genevieve stood in her doorway with a smirk on her face. "You're alive."

"You think I'd go out that easily?" There was no hostility in Sondra's tone, despite the dark look Genevieve gave her.

"No, I suppose not," Genevieve said, raising her head slightly. Her dark pixie cut lay flatter today than the first time I met her, but she still looked like she'd stepped out of a middle-aged women's fashion magazine. "What are you doing here? You know I refused to work with you again after—"

She cut off when Sondra shoved an envelope in her hands.

Genevieve raised a curious manicured brow. "What is this?"

"It's the debt I owe you," Sondra said simply. "All of it."

"Sweetheart, where could you possibly have…?" Genevieve trailed off when she opened the envelope and saw the number typed out on the cashier's check. She only let her surprise last a second before her face fell again. "I assume this isn't all you came for?"

"No," Sondra said. "We need your help."

Genevieve pressed her lips together. "Of course you do. Right this way."

She turned on her heel and left the door open for the rest of us to follow. The six of us filed down the hallway. I expected Genevieve to lead us into the door on the left like she had the last time I was here, but instead, she gestured to the room on our right.

We stepped into a sitting room dotted with Victorian-style furniture. A long red couch with a curved back sat opposite a large fireplace. Two matching black chairs sat on either side of that. The room was bathed in dark tones and lit only by two small lamps on end tables. An antique piano was situated next to an old grandfather clock. Large framed photographs and two huge mirrors hung from the walls.

"Please, have a seat." Genevieve sounded strangely pleasant. It was probably thanks to the giant check she'd just received. I resisted the urge to roll my eyes.

I sat between Venn and Fiona on the couch, while Sondra and Teagan claimed the chairs and Ryland sat on the piano bench. He no longer wore his sling, but he favored his left arm like it was still quite sore.

Genevieve stood in front of the empty fireplace. "Can I get you anything? Tea, perhaps?"

"Tea is fine," Sondra answered for everyone. I personally didn't care either way.

"Perfect." Genevieve snapped her fingers. "It should be ready shortly. Now, what can I help you with?"

Sondra leaned forward in her seat. "We're looking for information on an item called *Sapiens noctua,* or The Wise Owl. Have you heard of it?"

Genevieve nodded. "I have, but I must say I'm shocked to

hear that you have. Most people haven't heard of it, and those who have tend to write it off as myth."

"We hear you're in possession of the book that explains it," Teagan said.

Genevieve's lips twitched. "Who told you that?"

"That doesn't matter," Sondra said. "It's true, isn't it?"

Genevieve held Sondra's gaze for several seconds before motion by the door caught her eye. A pleasant expression washed over her face. "Ah, here's the tea."

A silver tray floated into the room. A teapot with seven cups sat upon it. We all watched as the tray slid onto the table in the corner by itself and the teapot began pouring tea into the cups. When the first finished, it floated through the air over to Sondra and landed gently in her hands. Sondra took a sip. It wasn't until we all had steaming cups of tea in our hands that Genevieve finally spoke.

"It's true. I am in possession of such a book, but it's not for sale."

"We're not here for the book," Ryland said. He hadn't even touched his tea.

I glanced to Venn, who was sipping his. I shot him a questioning glance, as if to ask if it was safe. Genevieve totally could've poisoned it. He gave a light nod, letting me know I could trust it. I took a sip. It was the most incredible tea I'd ever tasted.

"We're just here for the information in the book," Ryland clarified.

"Of course," Genevieve said, taking a sip of her own tea. "But with information this valuable, I must ask what you intend to use it for."

Sondra sighed. "You know me, Genevieve. Even *you* wouldn't use something like this for evil."

"Of course not," Genevieve scoffed. "Look around you. I have everything I could ever need. I have a beautiful home, more clients than I could ever dream of, and more wealth than you have in your pinky toe. And don't even get me started on my husband. He's a total dreamboat." Genevieve wiggled her eyebrows.

The gesture was weird, to say the least. Not to mention I was a little surprised to hear she was married. She seemed like the kind of person who would murder all four of her husbands for the money.

"If I wanted such an object," Genevieve said, "I would've found it by now. There's a reason I haven't divulged the information of its whereabouts."

"Why's that?" Fiona asked. She'd already finished her tea. She held her cup in her lap like she was hoping for more.

Genevieve took another sip. "Considering you know about The Wise Owl, you must know what kind of power it holds. No witch would want anyone else using that power on them. I have not gone after it because it is safest right where it is."

"That's exactly why we need to find it," Sondra insisted. "There's a vampire after it, and we believe he intends to use it to control who gets power and who doesn't. We hope to destroy it."

Genevieve's face fell. She dropped her teacup, but it hovered there in midair and glided back to the tray.

"Why you?" Genevieve asked skeptically. "Why should you be the ones to destroy it?"

We all exchanged a glance. No one knew how to answer the question.

"Why *not* us?" I blurted.

All eyes turned to me, including Genevieve's piercing stare.

"We've lost everything," I said. "Everything except each other. Our magic is one of the last things we have left. It's part of who we are. Come hell or high water, we're going to protect that—for everyone."

Sondra shot me an encouraging smile. She approved of my speech.

"You have a good point." Genevieve turned to Sondra. "I believe you will not use The Wise Owl for your own personal gain. What I do not know is if I can trust your colleagues and if you have enough power to retrieve the object on your own."

"You can trust us," Sondra promised. "All of us."

Genevieve pressed her lips together. "And what will you do with it once you find it?"

"Destroy it," Sondra said simply.

Genevieve sat there like a statue, contemplating our offer. "Okay. I will tell you, but should you fail, this is on *your* head. There's no going back."

"I know," Sondra said with confidence.

Venn ran his fingers across the back of my hand. I hadn't realized my hands had clenched around my teacup until then. I hadn't been sure we'd make it out of here with an answer.

From across the room, Genevieve snapped her fingers. The sound of a wooden chair against the hardwood floor reached my ears, and a chair immediately flew in through the door and stopped behind Genevieve. She sank into it casually, the skirt of her black dress lightly billowing around her. She snapped her fingers a second time. A leather-bound book floated in through the door, following her command. I remembered seeing the book sitting open on a table in the other room the last time I'd visited. I wrote it off as decoration. I was sorely mistaken.

Just as Amalia had described, the front leather cover was

stamped with an image of the moon eclipsing the sun and the stars scattered all around them. The book was huge, at least a foot and a half across and thicker than a stack of pancakes. The book floated gently into Genevieve's outstretched hands. She opened it to the index and began scanning the page, using her pointer finger as a guide.

"Mm…" she mused. "Let's see… ah, there it is."

She opened the book to the middle and flipped a few more pages until she found what she was looking for. We all held our breath, waiting to hear what she had to tell us.

Genevieve scanned the page. "The last known location of The Wise Owl was at a history museum in Minneapolis."

"That's it?" Teagan asked in disbelief. "That's the safest place for it? Out in the open?"

"That does seem strange," Sondra agreed skeptically. "Matias would've known where to find it by now."

"I assure you, it's not that easy to retrieve," Genevieve warned. "You will have to undergo grueling obstacles before it is yours."

Fiona leaned forward in her seat. "What exactly is it we're looking for? I mean, what *is* The Wise Owl?"

Genevieve blinked several times, like it was obvious. "It's a literal owl."

"Like, a stuffed owl?" Ryland asked.

Genevieve shot him an unamused glance. "No, a carving of an owl. You will know when you see it."

"Is that it?" Sondra peeked at Genevieve's book.

Genevieve snapped it closed. "That is all you need to know. When it comes to power like this, you can rest assured I would not lead you astray."

"I want to see the book for myself." Sondra wasn't demanding it. She was merely stating a fact.

Genevieve stood. "Sweetheart, this book has more secrets in it than you have past lives. Nobody touches the book but me."

"A book like that should belong to the public," Sondra argued.

"Not when there are people out there who would use it against others." Genevieve held her head high, confident in her reply.

It shocked me a little that Genevieve had a sense of morals. Venn had implied she was in to dark magic. She didn't seem like the kind of person to worry about others.

Genevieve snapped her fingers, and the teacups in everyone's hands rose and returned to their tray. I *had* to learn how to do that.

"That is all I can provide you at this time," Genevieve said. "If there's nothing else—"

"There is." Sondra rose from her chair. "I need to purchase some supplies for a protection spell."

Genevieve frowned. "Sweetheart, there are over a dozen different places in this city where you can buy protection spells. Why do you need me?"

"Because it's not just any protection spell," Sondra clarified.

Genevieve pressed her lips together. "Very well. Follow me."

It was clear in the look she shot us that the invite was only for Sondra. The rest of us remained seated and exchanged uncomfortable glances.

I was the first to speak. "Why does Genevieve care so much about protecting secrets? I thought she was a dark witch."

Venn leaned casually against the armrest of the couch. "I

told you, even dark witches have to believe in their cause to perform magic. I don't think she cares about protecting anyone else. I think there are things in that book that she's keeping secret to protect herself."

"Protect herself from what?" I asked curiously.

"Who knows?" Teagan asked rhetorically. "She's kind of had a shitty life. A lot of people have taken advantage of her. I can see where she might be paranoid."

"That's why she works in dark magic?" I asked. "Because she thinks it will protect her from…"

I wasn't sure I wanted to ask what would drive her down that road.

"From poverty, neglect, abuse…" Teagan shrugged. "Yeah, I guess."

Fiona opened her mouth to say something, but she stopped dead in her tracks when Sondra and Genevieve returned. Sondra held a small felt bag in her hands no bigger than her fist. We all stood. Venn was so close to me that I could feel the heat of his skin on mine.

"Thank you for your help, Genevieve," Sondra said genuinely. "And for trusting us."

Genevieve nodded, but a cold expression remained on her face. "Just be careful, okay?"

"We will," Sondra agreed.

"Excellent," Genevieve said. "Because this is not going to be an easy journey. Good luck."

8

───────────────

The clouds darkened above us when we arrived in the Twin Cities, casting an ominous glow across the entire landscape. It was evening, but the darkening sky made it seem several hours later than it actually was. Teagan and Ryland seemed completely relaxed as they walked across the museum parking lot in front of me. Fiona practically skipped along next to them, and Venn's hand was loosely tangled in mine. Beside me, Sondra looked nervous as she stared up at the building in front of us. The museum was the size of my high school with a long staircase leading up to Roman-inspired pillars at the entrance. The look on Sondra's face sent a wave of anxiety through my body.

"We have an hour until the museum closes," Ryland said, checking the clock on his phone. "Think we'll find it in time?"

Sondra took a breath. "We better. Because I'm not leaving here without it."

I like her attitude.

We climbed the steps and entered through the front door. The lobby was vast, with a ceiling that reached two stories high. A woman behind the front desk with wild curls and black framed reading glasses sold us our tickets, but not before warning us that the museum would be closing soon and that they didn't issue refunds. Venn just shot her a smile and assured her we'd be out by closing time.

"This way," Sondra hissed under her breath as soon as we had our tickets in hand. She led us out of the main lobby and into an exhibit hall on the right.

"How do you know where we're going?" I asked. "Shouldn't we split up to look for it?"

Sondra shook her head. "I can definitely feel something powerful in this building. Can't you?"

Apart from the footsteps following beside me, the hall was quiet. I concentrated, trying to feel the power she spoke of. Energy sizzled through the air. It was reminiscent of static electricity, but it was different. It was magic.

"I think I feel it," I admitted in a whisper.

"I don't feel anything," Fiona said.

"No," Sondra replied simply. "You wouldn't unless you were a witch."

Fiona frowned. "I'm working on it."

"I know," Sondra said with a smile. "A few more years and you'll be able to call yourself a low witch."

Fiona smiled back, like she was perfectly happy to settle with being a low witch. It seemed there was a lot I could learn from Fiona and her positive attitude. I had to make it a point to spend more time with her and soak up some of her positivity.

We wove through an endless maze of hallways and small rooms, each dedicated to a different era of history. Everyone went quiet as our eyes danced from display to display, looking for any signs of The Wise Owl. It felt like a half hour had passed, but I hadn't thought the museum was that big.

"I think we're getting close..." Sondra said as we entered a maze of rooms on the outer edge of the building. Each room was about the size of the hotel room we stayed at, with a window on one side and displays dotting the walls.

Sondra stopped in her tracks, and everyone paused behind her. She stared ahead through a doorway that led to the next exhibit hall. Past that, about fifteen yards from us, another doorway opened to a larger room. A life-sized stone carving of an owl sat perched atop a display pedestal.

Ryland furrowed his brow. "That was... easy to find."

"You're right," Sondra agreed. "This magic... it doesn't feel..."

My attention remained fixed on the Owl, so much that I barely heard what they said. My breath grew loud in my ears. The stone owl radiated magical energy. It danced across my skin in waves.

All that power... I could take it for myself. I sensed the thought go through my head, but it didn't feel like my own. I'd never wanted that kind of power. I just wanted to be me. If I was capable of more than I thought I was, that was something I would work for, not just steal from others.

No one should be able to take that hard work away from me... away from anyone, I thought. *We have to destroy it.*

The scent of smoke hit my nostrils, pulling me back to the present.

Teagan sniffed the air. "Does anyone else smell that?"

"Yeah—" I started to say.

Before I could finish my sentence, a shrill alarm cut through the air. The noise was so loud that we all jumped. I immediately brought my fists up, my eyes darting around the room. Teagan's hands flew to her waist, even though she'd had to leave her knives in the car due to the building's security regulations. The sprinklers on the ceiling opened up like the skies, raining water down on us. Ahead in the next room, orange light flickered across the walls.

A fire.

Ryland shouted something, but it was hard to hear him over the alarm blaring through the air.

"What?" Sondra screeched at Ryland.

"This must be one of the obstacles Genevieve mentioned," Ryland shouted. "We have to go through!"

"I don't know," Sondra screamed back with uncertainty. "I don't know that—"

"I'll go!" Fiona volunteered.

"No, Fiona!" Venn protested before she could shift.

Only a few seconds had passed, and the room in front of us was already engulfed in flames. They stretched into the air higher than my head, and dark smoke hit the ceiling and billowed out into the room we stood in. Heat radiated from the other room, and we all took a collective step backward.

"I'll shift into a fox," Fiona offered. "I'm small and can make it through."

"You could get hurt, Fiona," I objected. "I'll go through. I can fly."

"Everyone just calm down," Sondra demanded. "I think—"

"I can do this," Fiona argued. She shifted and darted between Ryland's legs and ran straight for the doorway and into the fire. Her red fur disappeared. Concern for her whipped through my body, and my heart hammered a million beats per minute.

"Fiona! No!" Ryland sprinted forward, with me, Venn, and Teagan close on his heels.

Sondra stood rooted in place and began mumbling an incantation under her breath.

We reached the doorway, but a blast of fire kicked into the room. A searing hot pain spread across my body as the flames touched my skin. I stumbled backward and nearly tripped over the feet behind me, but Venn caught me.

Sondra cursed. "The fire's working against me. That's not supposed to happen."

My eyes darted out the window for a second, but I didn't think anything of the darkening clouds until I did a double take.

"Oh my God," I whispered, horror filling my chest.

While Ryland and Teagan were preoccupied with finding a way through the fire and Sondra began a second incantation, Venn stepped forward to gaze wide-eyed out the window with me. Debris rushed past the glass. Things that shouldn't be flying through the air flipped across my vision: loose bits of concrete, entire tree branches, and a garbage can. In the middle of the debris, a funnel cloud had formed. It twisted and grew longer. All around us, the building began to shake.

I backed away from the window slowly and glanced to Sondra. "Is this another obstacle?"

Her eyes darted to the tornado beyond the window. She nodded and spoke breathlessly. "Yes. We need to destroy the Owl. Now."

"Forget the Owl!" Ryland shouted above the rattling of the building and the on-going fire alarm. "We need to save my sister!"

"She'll be fine!" Sondra cried. "The only way out of this is to get to the Owl."

The deafening sound of shattering glass exploding around us filled the air. I ducked. Venn was in front of me in a second, his strong abdomen pressed to the side of my head as he blocked me from the glass that sprayed across the room. The water raining down from the sprinklers had stopped, but strong winds swirled around us, whipping my hair in every direction. The flames seemed unaffected by the wind, but they continued to climb higher. Between the blaring fire alarm and the air pounding at my ears, I couldn't hear what Ryland shouted. When I lifted my head, all I saw was him run forward, disappearing into the wall of flames. Teagan followed behind him.

My eyes widened, and I sprang up out of Venn's protective hold. There was no way in hell they were entering that room without me. It was too loud to hear if Venn protested.

I shifted and flew into the air. I kept myself high, out of the reach of the flames, but visibility was nearly non-existent near the ceiling. I held my breath, knowing that if I inhaled, I wouldn't get any oxygen anyway. Heat seared my skin, making it feel as if my feathers were going to burn off, but I ignored it. There were more important things in life than feathers.

Glancing down, I saw nothing but orange flames through the thick smoke. I swooped lower, but I couldn't go far before the flames reached me. If I didn't get out of here soon, I was going to cook and be served on a platter for Christmas dinner. My lungs ached as I ran out of oxygen. On instinct, I inhaled a breath. My nasal passages burned, and my lungs felt heavy. I squinted across the room, but I couldn't see anyone anywhere.

I'm no use to them dead, I told myself.

One last glance through the flames revealed nothing. Both doors on either side of the room were completely engulfed in flames. I didn't hesitate, because I knew that if I did, I was done for. I flapped my wings and swooped downward, propelling myself through the door opposite the one I came in through.

My body collapsed to the tile floor, and I inhaled deep breaths, greedy for oxygen. My whole body shook, which was weird because I'd already caught my breath, and—

The sound of cannons exploded around me. Above my head, the ceiling fractured, alerting me to the fact that *I* wasn't the one shaking. The entire *building* was.

I spread my wings and shot into the air not a moment too soon. Plaster fell from the ceiling and smashed to the floor right where I'd been lying a moment ago. More pieces of plaster continued to rain down, and I dodged around them. I landed beneath the lip of one of the display tables for safety.

I finally took in the room. It was at least five times bigger than the other rooms we'd walked through. All types of stone artifacts lined the displays, with the carved owl sitting at the center of it all. I prayed my eyes would land upon Fiona, Ryland, or Teagan, but I saw no one.

Another piece of plaster cracked into the ground just in front of me. I jumped. If possible, my heart pounded even harder. My breathing grew erratic as my eyes darted from the flaming doorway to the crumbling ceiling.

Where are you? I silently begged. *Please be alive.*

The building moaned as the fracture in the ceiling widened. My eyes darted upward. These obstacles were insane.

The only way out of this is to get the Owl. Sondra's voice echoed in my head.

If this was all due to the magic in the Owl, then destroying it should stop all of this. I surveyed the crack in the ceiling, trying to decide if it was safe to dart across the room, grab it, and then get back under the safety of my table without injury.

Before I could make a move, four figures burst from the flaming doorway and fell into the room. Ryland cradled Fiona in her fox form, though she showed no signs of breathing. Beside him, Teagan screamed in pain. Most of her flesh was blackened with burns. Venn sat up and knelt over her. He said something I couldn't hear. I expected it was meant to comfort her.

I darted from the safety of my table the moment I saw them. But I never made it across the room. A loud rumble echoed across the space between us. My eyes just barely caught Venn's before a heavy wall of debris knocked his face out of view.

Sheer hopelessness slammed into my gut like a freight train. The pile of rubble had consumed them all.

They were gone.

9

"**N**O!"

My scream echoed off the walls of the museum. I hadn't even realized the violent winds had died down and the building was no longer shaking. The fire alarm had stopped blaring, but the pulse of blood in my ears seemed just as loud. It felt as if someone had reached into my abdomen and ripped my guts out.

In human form, I jumped onto the pile of rubble and began clawing at any pieces of broken building I could move.

"Rae!?" Sondra's voice cut through the air.

I glanced up to see the room between us was still on fire, but I couldn't see her through it.

"They're hurt!" I called back. "All of them!"

"They'll be okay," Sondra promised.

She has no idea.

"I need you to stay calm," she yelled across the space between us. "Can you do that?"

"I..." I wasn't sure I could, to be honest. *Calm* wasn't exactly my middle name, but I trusted Sondra. If we were going to make it out of here alive, she was my only hope. "I can try."

"Okay," she said in that soothing voice she always used. "This fire is enchanted. I can't get through. Is there another entrance to the room you're in?"

"Yeah!" I shouted back, while continuing to move debris out of the way. "There's another door that looks like the one I came through."

"Stay right there," Sondra instructed. "I'm going to come around."

A sliver of hope filled my heart, but it quickly disappeared as I dug further and further into the rubble without any signs of survivors.

"Hurry up!" I cried.

I quickly reminded myself to stay calm. I might need to use magic, and I couldn't do that if I was a blubbering mess. I took a deep breath and pushed a piece of concrete the size of a couch cushion out of the way. I inhaled a sharp breath when I saw Venn's face beneath me. Blood coated his forehead.

"Venn!"

His eyes fluttered open, and my heart soared in my chest. *He's alive!* Between the small opening of rubble, I bent and placed a kiss on his lips. It barely lasted a second, and I was too overwhelmed to truly enjoy it. It was too soon for this. Venn and I hadn't even had a chance to indulge in that make-out session he promised me.

"I'm going to get you out of here." My voice was strong. I couldn't let Venn see me weak right now.

"Wait," he croaked, stopping me from grabbing the next bit of rubble at the top of the pile.

I leaned over him. "What?"

He grimaced, like speaking caused him pain. "You can't save me, Rae."

"Of course I can," I argued. "I'm strong enough to move all this debris, and then I can heal you."

"No," he replied hoarsely. "You won't get to me in time."

"Stop talking," I demanded. "You're wasting time."

Venn spoke while I pushed pieces of concrete and plaster out of the way. "I've been impaled."

My face grew hot, but I forced down the lump in my throat. I had to stay calm as Sondra instructed.

"I need to tell you something," Venn said. "Rae, please stop and just listen to me. It's about your sister."

My entire body tensed, and I froze as he'd asked. "What about my sister?"

Venn took a deep breath. "She's dead."

I immediately backed off the pile to look him in the eye. He was wrong. "My sister's not dead. I would know."

"No," Venn argued. "You just want to believe it so badly that you won't face the truth. Clarita told me our search for Gregor Island was pointless because your sister was already gone. Jenna died that night the Soulless took her."

"You can't know that," I said with certainty. Except... how could I be sure? *My heart tells me she's alive* isn't much of an excuse. Clarita clearly had some serious powers. It was possible she could see into the past. "When did Clarita tell you?"

"It doesn't matter," Venn whispered through pained breaths.

"Don't you dare give up on me," I warned him. "I'm going to get you out of here and heal you."

Tears pricked at my eyes. If what Venn said was true, then I'd already lost my sister. I couldn't lose him, too.

"Forget about me," Venn insisted in a gravelly tone. "Matias is on his way. You have to keep going. You have to destroy the Owl before he gets to it."

Venn's eyelids fluttered.

"No, Venn," I ordered. "You aren't going to die."

I leaned down and pressed my lips to his again. They were so soft and warm, but he didn't respond to my touch. A hole opened in my chest.

"No, no, no," I repeated again and again.

No matter how much I didn't want to convince myself of the truth, I knew that Venn was gone. There was no hope of unearthing Fiona, Teagan, or Ryland alive, either. In the blink of an eye, I'd just lost everyone. I was alone now.

"Rae." Sondra's voice cut through the eerie silence.

My head snapped in her direction. I was suddenly reminded of the fact that I wasn't alone. Not entirely.

I shot to my feet. "Sondra, they…"

I didn't know how to break the news to her, but I didn't have to. She stepped forward and gazed into the rubble, straight at Venn's lifeless face. A hand shot over Sondra's mouth, and her eyes grew red.

"I'm sorry," I whispered.

She dropped her hand, but her eyes remained on him. "It's one thing to picture your worst fear in your head. It's another to actually experience it."

I bit my lower lip and nodded in agreement. I didn't think I could speak without turning into a sobbing mess.

You have to destroy the Owl. I could still hear Venn's voice in my head. There wasn't time for grief, not yet. Sondra and I still had work to do. In the meantime, I had to pick myself up and push forward.

This is going to suck balls.

"How do we destroy it?" I asked, my voice sounding stronger than I felt.

"I'm not sure," Sondra said, "but we have to try something."

"Okay," I agreed quickly.

I raced to the center of the room and snatched the Owl off its display. It was heavier than I thought it would be, but I held it above my head and hurled it at the tile floor with as much force as I could. It bounced off the floor and went spinning across the room. The tile had cracked and indented at the point of impact, but the Owl remained unharmed.

Sondra took a calm step forward. I took note of this and forced myself to relax, mirroring her stance, despite the agony ripping away at my insides.

"It's going to take a lot more than that to destroy this thing," Sondra stated, like it was fact.

"Any ideas?"

Sondra nodded. "A couple."

She faced the Owl, but remained frozen as it rose into the air under her silent command. It hovered three feet above my head. In the blink of an eye, it darted through the air and pummeled into the nearest wall. When that didn't work, Sondra sent it flying across the room at lightning speed and crashed into the opposite wall. The stone owl didn't even chip, though it left a sizable dent in the wall.

"I don't think this is going to work," I said. "It's too powerful."

Sondra guided the Owl to the ground on the other side of the room. "Let me try this..."

She muttered a syllable under her breath, and bolts of lightning erupted from her palms like I'd seen earlier during the ambush. Electricity sizzled through the air, sending strands of my hair to rise around me due to static. I wanted to join in, but I didn't know the incantation for lightning and didn't know if I'd be able to conjure it even if I did. Sondra's lightning bolts struck the stone over and over again, but it wasn't enough to crack it.

Smoke from the other room filled the air and burned my lungs. The fire roared, consuming the museum at an alarming rate.

"The fire!" I blurted. "You said it was enchanted. Maybe it's strong enough to destroy this thing."

One last bolt of lightning cracked through the air. Sondra paused for only a moment before lifting the Owl into the air with her magic. She sent it floating across the room and into the heart of the fire.

We stood side-by-side, watching the stone owl. Heat waves washed over us, and sweat broke out across my forehead. I expected to see the Owl crumble or melt or burn, but even though the flames were large and the smoke thick, I could see it remained unaffected.

My stomach bottomed out. If enchanted fire couldn't harm it, then what would?

"It's going to take the fires of hell to destroy this thing," I stated.

"I know," Sondra agreed. "It's too powerful."

She didn't have to remind me. Beneath the heat waves, I could still feel the Owl's power moving across my skin. It called to me like a beacon, begging me to take ahold of its powers and claim them as my own.

An idea suddenly struck me. "What if we weaken it?" I suggested. "If we take some power from it, it will be less protected, won't it?"

Sondra's gaze remained on the Owl in the fire. She stared at it intensely, as if willing it to explode. "It's too risky."

"But it's the only way," I countered. Somehow, I knew she'd agree with me. "I'll take its power, and you can destroy it."

"No," she countered, bringing her gaze to mine. "I'll take it. You don't know what that kind of power could do to you."

At this point, I was willing to take the risk if it meant keeping this thing out of Matias's hands.

"How do I destroy it, then?" I asked. "Sondra, I don't have that kind of power... not in this life. You're the only one who can destroy it. The least I can do is help weaken its power and give you a chance."

Sondra grimaced, contemplating my argument. "Okay, but you have to understand what you're getting yourself into."

I didn't. Not really. But whatever happened, I'd handle it.

"Bring it on," I said confidently.

Sondra guided the Owl out of the fire. It landed unharmed on the tile in front of us.

She stared at me seriously. "Don't let the power consume you, Rae. Everyone else is gone. I'm not going to lose you, too."

She hid the emotions from her tone, but I could see the heartbreak on her face. I swallowed my heartbreak, too.

"You ready?" she asked.

"Ready," I agreed.

"You know what you're doing?"

I didn't know how I knew, but the magic contained in the Owl sculpture told me exactly how to claim its energy as my own. I took a deep breath and bent to one knee. And then my hands clamped around the stone.

Red-hot pain seared across my skin. And it wasn't just because the stone was still blazing hot from the fire. This was a different kind of pain, the stabbing, scalding pain of magic that wasn't my own pouring into my body through my palms. And I licked it up like a chocolate milkshake through a straw. My scream echoed through the hall.

"Rae!" Sondra cried in concern. She reached out and touched my shoulder, and shock of a million volts burst down my arm.

I could feel her magic. This wasn't the minute charge I imagined she felt around other witches. It was sizzling hot, electric pain that felt as if I was standing in the eye of a thunderstorm. I could feel them all. All the witches, all the shifters, all the artifacts in existence. And I knew that by my simple command, I could flip off the switch to any one of them at will. The Wise Owl was more than just an artifact to control. It was a direct line to Synchrony. Anyone with malicious intentions could wreak serious havoc with this thing. It had to be the most dangerous weapon in the world.

And *I* had access to it. The possibilities flipped through my mind at lightning speed, but they went so fast that I could hardly process them. One thought stuck: I could do anything… *be* anything.

It'd be so easy.

Which is why it felt so wrong. Life wasn't easy. Life was an endless roller coaster ride with no destination. Sometimes it made you want to laugh and smile. Most times, it made you want to vomit.

This was one of those times when life was forcing my guts back up my throat. Whatever this power was, it wasn't *me*. I didn't want it. But more than that, I didn't want anyone else to have it.

"Rae," Sondra repeated, concern laced in her tone.

"Destroy… it…" I managed through gritted teeth.

Sondra's eyes widened as the ground began to shake

beneath our feet. She took several steps backward toward the pile of rubble.

The pile of rubble where Venn lay dead.

I squeezed my eyes shut, doing my best to push my grief down. I'd handle it later. Right now, I needed to focus on destroying this artifact before the magic in it destroyed me.

It should've destroyed me already, I told myself. There was a reason witches didn't try to handle magic above their skill level. But maybe this was different, since I was trying to harness the power rather than drain it.

An earth-shattering *crunch* filled the air.

"Rae!" Sondra cried to get my attention.

My gaze shot between us. A huge cavern had split the floor in two. I grabbed The Wise Owl and scurried backward, hugging the wall as the floor continued to crumble and the cavern grew. Above us, the crack in the ceiling widened to reveal the dark, clouded sky.

Sondra's eyes lit up. She shouted across the space between us. "Whatever you're doing, keep doing it!"

"I'm not doing anything," I assured her. Only trying to hold the magic in my body back.

"Yes, you are!" she called back. "We can do this together."

Sondra's lips moved, but I could no longer hear her over the sound of shattering earth around us. She continued to drift away from me as the rift between us widened. The rumbling of the earth was so strong that I was certain I was never going to hear again.

When it felt as if Sondra and I were miles apart, she caught my eye and yelled something at me. There was no way in hell I could hear her from here, so I tried to read her lips. I was a terrible lip reader.

She pointed to the Owl and then gestured to the cavern.

Was she suggesting I throw it in? What would that do if smashing it hadn't worked before?

She continued to point at the cavern. It looked like she was encouraging me to gaze into it. Slowly, I got to my hands and knees, though it was difficult to maintain my balance as the earth rocked around me.

Daringly, I peeked over the edge. Dirt and rock stretched down for miles, ending in a red glowing pit.

Holy shit! The earth's crust had broken apart to reveal a layer of magma.

"Throw it!" I just barely heard Sondra's instructions carry through the wind.

I hesitated. I could keep The Wise Owl—keep all the power for myself.

No, I countered instantly. I wouldn't take that power from everyone else.

I heaved the heavy stone up in my arms and then hurled it over the edge of the cavern. I watched it tumble over and over again, until it became just a small dot and then disappeared from view completely. I knew the moment it hit the magma because I felt its power *whoosh* out of me.

And then everything went black.

10

I lay on my back. The earth was perfectly still, and the white ceiling above me had been untouched by any natural disaster. My head spun.

What the—?

I pushed myself to my elbows and glanced around the quiet exhibit hall. Five bodies lay sprawled on the floor beside me. The next room was pristine, as if it hadn't been burning just moments ago. I was so confused that I could hardly process the images in front of me.

The sound of clapping reached my ears. My head snapped in the direction of the opposite doorway just as a woman in a black dress stepped through it.

"Well done, Rae," she said. "I'm impressed."

Reality came crashing down on me. It took my breath away, and not because I was upset. I was beyond *relieved*. It wasn't real. None of it. Tears sprang to my eyes.

Beside me, everyone else began to wake. Venn sat up. Though confusion filled his eyes, they were full of life. Happiness swept through me and consumed the very core of my soul.

I sprang to my feet and tackled Venn with a hug. "You're okay!"

He squeezed me back so hard I thought he might crack a rib, but I didn't care. I just wanted to feel his arms around me.

He nuzzled his face in my hair. "Of course I'm okay. I thought I'd lost you!"

"Me?" I drew away in surprise.

"Yes," he said, tears brimming his eyes. "The ceiling collapsed on you. It felt so real."

I bit down hard on my lower lip and shook my head. "In my version, you were the one who died. All of you except Sondra."

Venn pushed my hair out of my face and stared longingly into my eyes. My heart cartwheeled around in my chest under his gaze.

"So, that thing you said about my sister…?" I asked. "It wasn't true?"

Venn's brow furrowed. "What thing?"

Thank God!

I whirled around, shooting daggers at Genevieve. "What did you do to us?"

She smiled and stepped further into the room. Her heels clicked against the tile. "Relax. You did exceptional."

"That was a nasty-ass prank," Teagan bit from behind me.

Sondra stood and spoke calmly. "It was a test."

Genevieve stopped in the middle of the room and crossed her hands in front of her. She smiled a knowing smile.

I glanced between Sondra and Genevieve. "You knew." It wasn't a question.

Sondra nodded, never tearing her gaze from Genevieve. "I

suspected something wasn't right, but I didn't realize Genevieve was behind it. I tried to tell you, but when you didn't hear me out, I figured the best thing to do was go with it. The vision wasn't going to end until we destroyed the artifact."

Ryland helped Fiona to her feet and pulled her into a hug. It was like watching ghosts. The vision had felt so real.

"Precisely," Genevieve confirmed.

"At some point, our visions must've diverged, showing us each our worst fears," Sondra theorized as Venn and I stood.

Ryland leveled his gaze on Genevieve. "You better have a damn good excuse for doing this. That was beyond cruel."

Genevieve pursed her lips. "I may break the rules every once in a while, but I am not cruel. Not without purpose, at least."

Fiona crossed her arms. Even *she* wasn't taking any of this shit. "So, why exactly did you have to make us watch everyone we love die?"

"To test you," Genevieve said simply.

"Test us for what?" Teagan demanded. "You already know what we're capable of."

Genevieve shook her head. "The Wise Owl is a very delicate artifact. It requires much more than experience to get to. I had to know if your team was capable. If you couldn't make it through this, you'd never make it through the real thing."

"And we passed?" There was almost no emotion in Sondra's voice.

"Yes," Genevieve said proudly. "You were each shown your worst fears to test your resilience—how quickly you could bounce back from hardships. You're going to need it when you undergo the true obstacles. Only one of you failed."

She shot a look at Fiona, who dropped her head in shame.

"You were then each tested on your intentions, how well you could resist the power of The Wise Owl. Only one of you passed."

Genevieve looked at me. I glanced around, wondering if she was looking at someone behind me, but everyone was now standing side by side. Surely she didn't mean that I was the only one who could resist the power.

Genevieve pressed her lips together in thought and stared at me. "Strange, though. I designed the deception to replicate the powers of the true artifact. You shouldn't have felt as much connection to Synchrony as you did. You should've only had the power to block magic, not steal it."

I glanced to Sondra, wondering if she could explain what that meant, but she looked as confused as I did.

Genevieve waved her hand nonchalantly. "No matter. You were still able to resist the power. That's good enough for me, but it means that if I am to trust you in the location of the true artifact, you must all promise that Rae will be the one to retrieve it. The rest of you will act to protect her through the obstacles."

"Why trust us at all?" Sondra asked skeptically. "You never have in the past."

Genevieve pursed her lips. "Because I agree with you. This power should not exist. Everyone should have a right to their own magic. I would destroy it myself... if I thought that I could. But we both know I couldn't resist magic like that, not once it was in my hands. And so, I need you to do it for me."

Understandable, I guess.

"But next time, you need to be more prepared," Genevieve warned. "I guarantee that when you face the Artifact for real, the earth isn't just going to open up and swallow it whole."

"Does your book mention how to destroy it?" Sondra asked. "The real Artifact?"

"It'll take more witches than you have at your disposal," Genevieve said. "This artifact was not created alone, nor can it be destroyed alone. There is strength in numbers, and you're going to need a helluva good team of witches to disperse the power it holds."

Sondra jutted her chin out confidently. "We can work with that."

Genevieve nodded her approval.

"Is any of this real?" I asked, gesturing around the exhibit hall. "Or are we still sitting in your lounge with teacups in our hands?"

Genevieve's laughter reverberated off the walls of the museum. "Yes, this is real. I do not have the power to produce visions on my own. I needed a bit of… help."

Her eyes locked on something behind me. I turned to stare past the open doorways. A stone carving of a coiled snake sat on the display where the Owl had been in my vision. The strong tingles of magic I'd felt earlier danced across my skin.

"This is the artifact responsible for your visions," Genevieve explained. "I arrived an hour ahead of you to ensure you would only see what I wanted you to see. Obviously, you didn't all pass my test, but that would be nearly impossible. It's clear to me that you all care very deeply for one another, and I'm confident that you will make a good team."

She was right. We did care deeply about each other.

Genevieve sighed. "Having said that, it's time to tell you the truth."

11

I remained speechless the whole time Genevieve explained the truth to us.

"The true Artifact is hidden in a cave," she'd said.

Of-freaking-course it was. The top of a mountain or the bottom of the ocean, I was down with. Why did it have to be a cave? They were dark, damp, and creepy. Worst of all, they had very few escape routes, and that was the part that scared me most.

"A group of witches brought The Wise Owl to the States sometime in the early 1800s," Genevieve told us. "They wanted to make sure it wouldn't fall into the wrong hands but didn't want to destroy it in case they had to use it to protect the world from a vengeful witch. After years of hiding it and searching for the best solution, they laid it to rest in a cave that remains unexplored to this day."

She wanted us to explore the bloody cave.

I, apparently, was the only one bothered by the idea of a spelunking expedition. Who knew what could happen to us?

We could get lost and starve to death. The whole thing could cave in and trap us there. We could suffocate.

I couldn't exactly back out now, though, not when Genevieve assured us that I was the only one who could resist its power and destroy it for good.

I worried about Jenna, and my mind continued to flicker to the map Clarita had given us. But I couldn't get what Clarita had said out of my mind, about how we had to finish our current quest first before going after my sister. Every fiber of my being told me to say screw it and race off to Gregor Island on my own, but another part of me—my intuition, perhaps—told me that I should listen to Clarita. Maybe it had something to do with being the only one who could resist The Wise Owl's power.

I didn't know. Frankly, I didn't know anything these days, and it put me completely on edge.

Genevieve was deliberately vague on the details, saying that the less we knew, the better. She offered to sponsor our journey, which meant booking us a five-star suite in the Twin Cities while she got the rest of our affairs in order.

"You need to rest," she'd said. It sounded like she honestly cared about our well-being. I was starting to think that Genevieve wasn't all that bad, that there was a good heart hidden beneath all the black lace and dark makeup.

And a crapload of money, too, I thought as the six of us stepped inside our hotel room.

Hotel room was a massive understatement. It was a freaking royalty suite. My jaw dropped to the floor. Fiona went bug-eyed beside me.

"Holy moneybags," Ryland muttered under his breath.

A vast room bathed in beige tones stretched out in front of us and met up with a row of floor-to-ceiling windows. On the other side of them, a balcony overlooked the city, which was hauntingly beautiful beneath the dark night sky. Two long couches faced a flat-screen TV that practically took up the whole wall. Another seating area surrounded a gas fireplace. Beside that, six chairs sat around a dining room table next to a full kitchen and bar.

I managed to tear my gaze from the main room and glanced into one of the bedrooms. A huge king-sized bed took up the space. On the opposite wall, a smaller TV hung above another fireplace. A private bathroom sat beyond an open door.

"Ohmigosh!" Fiona called from another room. "You have to see this."

I whirled around and almost slammed straight into Venn's chest. I stumbled backward. He stared down at me with a soft smile, like he wanted to say something.

"We get this room!" Teagan called, pushing past us and breaking our stare. She dropped her bag on the king bed.

"Rae, come look!" Fiona popped her head out of one of the doors and gestured for me to follow her.

I dropped my gaze shyly, wondering what Venn was about to say to me, but I stepped away from him and followed Fiona.

In the main part of the suite, Sondra held the small black bag Genevieve had given her. She pulled a pinch of a powdered substance from it and mumbled under her breath as she sprinkled it in the corner of the room.

"Come on," Fiona encouraged. She led me into a huge bathroom, complete with a glass-door shower with a rain-fall showerhead. Beside that sat a jetted tub fit for at least two.

Venn and I could fit.

Wait. Where had that thought come from? *Hold your horses, girl. You haven't even got to second base yet.*

Still, the tub looked inviting. I couldn't remember the last time I actually took a decent bath, considering my apartment only had a shower, sans tub. I longed to fill it and let the jets massage away all the tension I'd been bottling up these past few years. It wouldn't hurt to spoil myself, would it?

"Dibs on the tub!" I blurted.

Fiona laughed. "Come on. Let's go check out the other rooms."

The last room was a double queen suite. I did the calculations in my head, and unless Venn decided he wanted to sleep on the couch, we were going to end up in bed together again. Which I had absolutely *no* qualms about. I mean, it wasn't like we were going to *do* anything with Sondra and Fiona in the same room, but that didn't matter as long as I got to snuggle up in his arms again.

But first, I was getting in that jet tub.

"Genevieve said we could order anything from room service and charge it to the room," Sondra announced. She flipped through a menu on the coffee table. "Anyone hungry?"

"I'll eat later," I told her. "I'm really itching to get in that tub."

Sondra's eyes lit up. "That bathroom is amazing, isn't it? Oh, hey. When you get out, do you want me to do a cleansing spell on your clothes? It'll save you at least an hour on laundry."

"That would be amazing," I agreed.

I slipped into the bathroom while everyone else continued to explore the suite. Inside, I took a deep, calming breath. Tomorrow, I would worry about Matias, the Artifact, and the Soulless. Tonight, I was going to relax.

After a beat, I crossed the room and twisted the faucet. Warm water rushed out of the tap and filled the base of the tub. A neatly-arranged stack of toiletries sat on a washcloth on the ledge. I rifled through it and found a travel-sized bottle of bubble bath. After twisting off the cap, I turned the bottle completely upside down and let the whole thing pour into the water. Bubbles erupted under the flow of the water. Satisfied, I turned to the switch on the wall and dimmed the lights before stripping off my clothes. I would've started soothing music on my phone if I had it, but I'd left it at my apartment the night we fled Nocton.

I climbed into the hot water and leaned my head back against the edge of the tub. The warmth seeped into my bones and eased the tension in my muscles. When the water reached my chest, I turned off the faucet and started the jets. Bubbles grew higher and higher, and the jets massaged away the rest of my tension.

It felt like a sin to soak in the tub when the rest of the world was drowning in turmoil. I bet there were vampires roaming the city streets right now who deserved a stake to the heart. And it wasn't fair that I was sitting here warm in a tub when I had a lead on Jenna's whereabouts and wasn't doing a damn thing about it.

There's nothing you can do right now, I reminded myself. *Relax while you can.*

With that, I inhaled deep breaths, taking in the lavender scent of the bubbles. For once, my mind wasn't racing. I focused only on the rise and fall of my chest and the image of dark brown eyes—Venn's eyes—behind my lids. I couldn't remember the last time I'd felt this relaxed. It must've been years.

I stayed in the tub for what felt like at least an hour, but it still didn't seem long enough. I finally decided to get out when most of the bubbles had fizzled away and the water temperature had dropped to lukewarm. I lathered shampoo through my long dark hair, then added conditioner and scrubbed the rest of my body with soap before getting out. I was disappointed that I didn't get a chance to shave, considering my legs were starting to look like a gorilla's and my pits were in serious need of a razor. That *definitely* meant nothing could happen between Venn and me anytime soon.

After I'd dried off, I twisted the towel around my head and slipped into the plush white robe hanging from the back of the door. At the sink, I took a swig of complimentary mouthwash and swished it around in my mouth. Then I gathered my clothes from the floor and stepped out into the main room.

The suite was quiet and empty. I glanced into both bedrooms, but the beds were still neatly made, and nobody was in there. I spun around, wondering where they'd all gone without telling me, but then my eyes settled through the glass doors and onto the balcony. Sondra sat curled up on one of the patio chairs.

"Hey," I said gingerly as I stepped out onto the balcony and pulled up a chair beside her.

She looked up from the notepad she'd been doodling on. "Hey. You ready for that cleansing spell?"

"Yeah. Where is everyone?"

Sondra set her notepad aside. "They're down at the pool."

I couldn't help but steal a glance at her drawing. It was clearly just a quick sketch, nothing like the detailed drawings I'd seen on the wall back at her house, but she was amazingly talented. Somehow, she'd managed to capture the shadows perfectly on the face she'd drawn.

"That looks like Matias," I observed.

Sondra took my clothes and began shaking them out to fold them. "Yeah. I'm trying to see if I can remember him."

"Like, from a past life?" I asked while adjusting my robe to cover my knees.

"Yes. Sometimes, I think I recognize him, but I'm not sure. It's hard to tell with the silver eyes. But I think there might be something to my theory of him being a witch before he changed. It's like the memory of him is right on the edge of my mind, but I can't quite grab it yet." Sondra finished folding my clothes and placed them in a pile on her lap. "Drawing helps me with the memories."

I smiled. "You're really good, by the way. I saw the drawings at your house."

"Oh, you did?" she asked in a bright tone.

"Yeah, I thought they were great. I can't draw, so I'm not sure how I'll ever remember my past lives."

Sondra's brow creased. "It's not the same for everyone. Drawing helps me, but you'll find something else that'll help you."

"Like what?" I asked. "How does remembering this stuff work?"

Sondra shrugged. "It usually starts with some sort of trigger, like seeing someone you met in a past life, visiting a place you'd been in that life, or doing something that would've been significant to you."

"Shouldn't I remember my life as Abigail now that I've met Venn?"

Sondra shook her head. "Not necessarily. It's not normal to remember your past lives. It takes magic."

I frowned and mumbled, "Which I'm not very good at."

Sondra looked shocked by my attitude. "Don't say that. It just takes practice."

I sighed, knowing she was right. "How do you stay so calm and positive all the time?"

Sondra pressed her lips together and looked out over the city. "I guess I just trust Synchrony. I know that things will always work out, so it's easy to let go of worry."

"You worry about your family," I pointed out.

She smiled. "Of course I do. I don't want to lose them. Sometimes you just can't help but worry about the things that matter most to you."

My thoughts flew to Jenna, and a pang of guilt shot through my chest. I shouldn't have ever given up on her. I shouldn't have waited two years for a Soulless to show up on my doorstep and force me into taking action.

"I know what you mean," I whispered. "Could you maybe teach me? How to do magic, I mean?"

"I can teach you the basics," she offered, sending my heart soaring. "But the true magic comes from within you."

"I know," I said. "I don't expect you to do any of the work for me, just... I guess teach me how to stop doubting myself. Venn says that's what's holding me back."

Sondra nodded. "He's right. Doubt only breeds negativity. Synchrony reflects your intentions back on you, so if you doubt yourself, you will only see negative results."

"Venn explained that to me," I said, leaning further back in my chair. "I guess I'm just not sure how to do it, to let go of the doubt and be more positive."

Sondra and I stared at the city lights without saying anything for several breaths. Finally, she spoke.

"I wish I could tell you there's a secret to it, but I can't. It's something you have to figure out on your own, unfortunately." She scooted her chair around a few inches to look at me. "There are two things I've done to improve my magic. The first"—she held up a finger—"is to breathe." She inhaled a long, deep breath to demonstrate.

I raised an eyebrow. "That's it? Just *breathe?*"

Her lips turned down. "When you put it that way, it sounds silly, but I swear by it. With each breath I take, I release the tension from my shoulders and the negative energy with it. You just have to find what works for you."

"Well, the bath helped calm me, but I can't take a bubble bath every time I want to perform magic," I said.

Sondra nodded in agreement. "It's a lot easier said than done. Magic can be simple, but that doesn't mean it's easy. We'll have to figure something out for you. I suggest starting with a happy memory."

"Okay," I agreed, thinking on it briefly. "What's the second thing?"

"I don't do it as much anymore, only when I successfully execute a spell or potion I've never done before, but the second thing I do is take notes."

"Take notes?" Magic couldn't be this easy. If it was, everyone would be doing it.

"Yes," she said. "If you believe you're good at magic, you will see all the times you succeed. If you believe you're bad at magic, you'll see all the times you fail. I want to believe I'm good at magic, so I keep a record of my successes."

I considered it for a moment. "I think Fiona was trying to explain this to me before. She said I was good at healing because I'd already done it before. I already *believe* I can do it."

"Right." Sondra nodded. "Every success will make you believe that much more. Eventually, you won't need to remind yourself to believe in it. You'll have looked at enough evidence that you aren't just temporarily convinced; you'll truly have faith."

A sense of peace washed over me, though that could've been residual feelings left over from my amazing bath. I was starting to think I understood this. Enough to get a good start on practicing my magic, anyway.

"What do you want to believe?" Sondra asked curiously.

I kept my eyes on the city lights and didn't meet her gaze. What *did* I want to believe? I wanted to believe Jenna was alive. I wanted to believe Matias wouldn't get his hands on the Artifact. I wanted to believe that one day life would be better than it was now.

But I didn't want to say any of that. I sensed Sondra wasn't looking for me to dive that deep. Instead, I settled with, "I want to believe that I'm powerful, that I'm capable of more than just healing. I mean, healing is great, but I feel like I could do so much more."

A smile crept across Sondra's face. "Have you ever done a cleaning spell, Rae?"

I shook my head.

Her smile widened, radiating positive energy across the balcony. "Today's your lucky day." Sondra stood and gestured for me to follow her inside. "It's actually a really easy spell. We just need something that signifies cleanliness."

"Would a bottle of shampoo work?" I asked.

"That would be perfect," Sondra said.

She set my pile of clothes on the coffee table while I slipped into the bathroom to grab the shampoo off the lip of the tub.

"Okay," Sondra said, patting the couch cushion beside her to encourage me to sit. "You'll have to use a small amount of shampoo and rub it on your hands. Then you'll place them over the clothes and repeat after me."

"That's it?" I asked as I sat beside her.

"That's it," she replied simply. "I told you it was easy."

I followed Sondra's instructions and repeated the short incantation. I didn't even feel the magic buzz through me. By the end of the incantation, I wasn't sure the spell took.

"Did it work?" I asked. "I barely felt anything."

Sondra shrugged. "Do you believe it did?"

I hesitated. "I—I'm not sure."

"Check," she instructed.

I grabbed my jeans off the pile first. To my surprise, they were soft, like they'd just come out of the dryer, and they smelled of lavender. I unfolded them to see that the dirt on them was completely gone.

"Wow." I was practically speechless. I mean, I knew this spell wasn't very advanced, but still, I did it. A sense of pride washed over me.

I pulled the jeans to my chest and turned to Sondra. "Thank you so much! I should probably go get dressed. This robe is a little... airy. I don't need to be flashing my goods to everyone when they get back."

Oh, wow. I'd taken that a step too far. I barely knew Sondra, and here I was talking about my *goods*. Awkward.

I gathered the rest of my clothes, but I hesitated before I stood.

"What?" Sondra asked curiously.

I bit my lower lip. "You wouldn't happen to know any sort of hair removal spell, would you?"

Sondra held back a laugh. "No, but I know Fiona has a package of disposable razors in her bag and wouldn't mind you using one. I'll get one for you."

Sondra rose from the couch. As I watched her leave, I realized I had a question for her that I never got a chance to ask.

I shot to my feet before she left the room. "Hey, Sondra?"

She turned around, her hand on the door frame to our room, and stared expectantly at me. "Yeah?"

"I was just wondering… you don't have to answer if you don't want to. But why didn't you pass Genevieve's test?"

Sondra paused. "I guess even though I don't want anyone else to have the power… I feel like I could still use it for good."

With that, she left the room.

12

Ten minutes later, I returned to the bedroom with silky soft legs. I'd kept the white robe on because it was plush, comfortable, and I'd rather sleep in it than in my jeans, though I'd added clean underwear beneath it. Thank God. I no longer felt like anything was at risk of going on display. I ran my fingers through my damp tangles. Seeing as I didn't have a hairbrush with me, it was the best I could do.

The sound of the front door opening met my ears. Hopefully it was Fiona. I could ask if she brought along a hairbrush.

"Shut up, Ryland," I heard Teagan scold lightheartedly. "You need to watch less TV and read more books like Venn does."

"What's the difference?" Ryland retorted. "They're both fiction. My method is easier."

"It kills more brain cells," Fiona teased.

"And reading doesn't?" Ryland asked.

"Really?" Venn asked lightheartedly. "Of all the things you could make fun of me for, you choose to take a jab at *reading*. You're really stretching it there."

"What else am I going to tease you for?" Ryland asked. "Playing the guitar? Chicks dig that kind of thing. The only other thing I've got is the race card, and—"

"Don't you dare," Fiona scolded him before Ryland could say anything about Venn's skin color.

I stepped into the doorway to see Ryland holding his hands up in surrender.

"I wasn't going to," he said.

My eyes fell on Venn. I couldn't tear my gaze away from him even if I wanted to. He wore only a pair of black athletic shorts, which left his broad shoulders and defined abs exposed. Though he'd clearly dried off since leaving the pool, several water droplets remained on his skin. I suddenly felt like my robe was tied too tight, like it was stealing the air from my lungs. I was getting *far* too warm wrapped in the plush fabric.

Fiona's eyes caught mine. "Oh, good. You're out of the bath. I'm next."

Fiona hurried into the open bathroom. She wore a black sports bra with matching athletic shorts. I guessed her swimsuit never made it into her luggage. Teagan was the only one dressed in a proper swimsuit, an olive-green bikini that suited her tan complexion and showed off every curve.

A pang of jealousy hit my gut at the sight of her thin legs, flat tummy, and generous bosom. Why Venn wanted pasty-white *me* when he lived with *her*, I'd never know. But he didn't even steal a glance her way. Which was weird, because even *I* was staring at her breasts and contemplating my sexuality.

When my eyes returned to Venn's strong, defined torso, Teagan's boobs completely fell from my mind. There was a good chance I was drooling at this point, but I didn't care. I could stare at him all night, entranced, and not get bored.

"Rae," Venn said as he approached me.

"Huh?" I asked in a daze, my eyes still greedily drinking him in.

"My eyes are up here."

At that, I instantly snapped out of it. Right. He was a human being, not some object on display.

My cheeks flamed. "Sorry. I just—"

"I was kidding," he said with a smile, stopping just inches from me in the doorway.

He reached out to sweep a strand of wet, tangled hair behind my ear. I gazed into his brown eyes, and my heart did that fluttery thing in my chest again. I stood there frozen, my cheek tingling in the spot where he'd touched me. My throat felt like sandpaper when I finally reminded myself to swallow.

"Seriously," Teagan said from the couch, pulling mine and Venn's attention away from each other. "Stop making googly eyes at each other and get a room already."

Venn gave her the side eye. "We have a room, thank you very much."

He stepped forward and pulled me inside the bedroom before shutting the door behind us. I stifled a laugh, but it quickly died when my eyes met his again. A single lamp between the beds lit up the room, casting shadows across his gorgeous face.

My God. What was it about looking this man in the eyes? The way he constantly gazed at me in wonder took my breath away. It was as if he had some sort of magic that stalled my heart but sent it beating a million times per minute all at the same time. My brain turned to mush around him, I swear. When he looked at me, nothing else in the world seemed to matter.

Which was dangerous as hell. Luckily for me, I liked danger.

But *this*? This love-sick, heart-on-fire girl wasn't me. Venn changed everything I knew about myself. He made me want to tear all my walls down for him. And for some strange, inexplicable reason, that didn't scare me when it should.

Venn smiled down at me, a seductive smile that sent my heart *pitter-pattering* against my chest.

Like I said, *so* not me.

"Now that we have a room, what should we do with it?" he whispered softly. He stood so close that I could feel his body heat, though he didn't touch me.

Which I was desperate to remedy. Without thinking, I reached out and placed my fingertips to his exposed chest. I studied his smooth skin, marveling at his even skin tone. Even the goosebumps that grew beneath my touch were beautiful.

I knew what *I* wanted to do with the room. My body screamed for it as certain parts I never used heated.

I bit my lower lip and lifted my gaze. He stared down at me with an expectant half-smile. He was waiting for me to say it out loud.

Ugh. Why did we have to use *words*? Wasn't it obvious? Couldn't he feel the heat sizzling between us? Or maybe it was just the robe. He'd have to help me out of it before I fainted from heat exhaustion.

Virgin, I teased myself. Seriously, what was *wrong* with me?

Venn was experienced. He'd never mentioned it directly, but the way he'd talked about being a blood slave hinted that there was more to that story. I wouldn't have been surprised if he'd lost his virginity long before that. I wasn't going to ask all the details, because I knew it would only resurface old, bitter memories. While it stung a little to think about him with other girls—with *Maliya*—it also made me want to make him forget about all of that. If I could, I'd kiss all the pain from his past away.

"We could... finish what we started in the elevator," I finally answered.

Oh, God. Why did he make me say it out loud?

"Mm..." Venn said in a tone that made my knees go weak. "I think that can be arranged."

In the blink of an eye, Venn swooped down and pressed his lips to mine. Butterflies danced in my stomach like a freaking rave party, and every inch of my skin came alive.

My arms slid around his neck as he deepened the kiss. I barely realized we were moving across the room until the back of my legs bumped up against the bed. I expected to tumble backward, but Venn caught me and twisted. He fell onto the mattress on his back and pulled me on top of him. My eyes roamed his body, and his dropped to my chest, where my robe had parted slightly.

"I can't believe how natural it feels to be with you," I said.

Why did I have to break the silence? We were doing fine without talking. Stupid mouth.

"You mean... almost like we're soulmates?" he asked.

A wide smile spread across my face. "Exactly."

The word *soulmates* hung in the air and permeated down into my bones. I couldn't explain it, but beyond a shadow of a doubt, I knew that Venn was it for me. It made no rational sense, but I didn't think it had to, as long as I trusted it was true.

Venn pulled me closer to him and pressed his lips to the sensitive skin below my ear. My back arched in response to his touch, and I held back a moan as his lips traveled down my neck, his breath brushing across my skin the whole way.

He drew away. "What do you want, Rae?"

You. All of you.

"I mean, I know it feels right to be with you," he said, "but we can take this as fast or slow as you want. I don't want you to feel rushed just because—"

I silenced his words with a passionate kiss. Heat pooled in my belly. We both drew a deep breath when we parted.

"Believe me," I said, "I'm not waiting for anything, except maybe a private room." I shot a glance at the door, which didn't have a lock on it. Anyone could barge in at any moment.

Venn's eyes widened. "I didn't mean—I just meant—"

"It's okay," I told him with a giggle. "I'm fine with just this."

Liar.

He stared up at me with desire and passion in his eyes. He pushed himself up briefly to place a kiss on my nose. "You're amazing. You know that? Has anyone ever told you you're amazing?"

The question was rhetorical, but I answered anyway. "I don't think so. I mean, besides my parents, but that was in, like, a totally different way. And, I mean, pretty much everyone who called me the Ravenite, but they thought I was some sort of super shifter or something."

Oh my God. You're ruining it with your rambling.

"I'll shut up now," I said quickly.

Venn laughed. "You're great."

The words sent a warm tingle to settle in my chest. I felt light and airy, carefree.

"So, uh..." I threw another glance at the door. "Sondra and Fiona aren't going to stay out there all night. I want to enjoy every second of alone time I have with you."

Venn wiggled his eyebrows. "Better get started then."

I beamed and accepted his invitation. My lips trailed from his mouth and down his jaw, then to his neck and finally to his collarbone. He shivered beneath my touch, and his hands tightened from where they rested on my hips.

I'm such a tease.

Tonight would take me further than I'd ever been with a guy, and I should've been terrified. But with Venn—with his kisses and his hands roaming over my backside—I wasn't scared. I didn't want to tease him. I wanted to take this further. Not all the way… but further.

I arched my back and pressed my pelvis into his. Slowly, I reached up with shaky fingers and tugged at the tie on my robe. The fabric fell away to expose my bare midriff and my bra. My breasts swelled as he gasped, his hungry eyes drinking me in. His hands moved over the bare skin of my legs and ran all the way up my abdomen until his fingers settled against the fabric on the underside of my bra. My mouth went dry, and my blood pulsed in my ears. What was he waiting for?

He couldn't wait any longer. He let out a deep growl, and he sprang on me. His arms were around me in an instant, dragging me into him until our lips connected. My mouth parted, letting him in. His tongue danced across mine, and I gladly welcomed the rush it brought. It was like conjuring magic, only a hundred times more powerful. Unlike magic, the tingle didn't shoot straight through me. It gathered into a ball in my chest, making me feel heavy and light all at the same time.

Venn spun me around, tossing me on my back. He paused a moment as his eyes roamed over me. My chest heaved in heavy breaths as I waited in unbearable anticipation for his next move.

Venn grabbed the sheets from beneath me, and we both climbed under the covers. He bit his lower lip as he hovered above me, straddling me. His gaze flickered down to my breasts. Desire burned in his eyes, reflecting back how I felt.

Now it was my turn to run my hands up his legs. Brazenly, I pushed the fabric of his shorts aside and ran my hands up to the skin at the apex of his thighs. The ends of my fingers just barely grazed him *there*. He was *so* ready for me.

"What do you want, Rae?" he whispered.

I thought about it for a moment. The part of my soul connected to him wanted it *all*. But the Rae part of me—the inexperienced part—begged for merely just a taste. We didn't have any protection on hand, which was kind of a deal breaker for me. But there was *plenty* we could do without it.

"I want you to touch me," I whispered back before wrapping my arms around his neck and pulling him closer to me. My chest heaved, and my nipples hardened beneath the fabric of my bra. "And kiss me."

Venn gladly took my invitation, claiming my mouth as his own once again. My legs wrapped around his middle, pulling him even closer to me, while my hands ran across the exposed skin on his back. His right thumb ran just below my underwire, teasing me.

Do it.

Venn wrapped an arm underneath me and pinched the sides of my bra clasp together. Suddenly, the fabric loosened, and cool air rushed across my exposed breasts. Venn pushed aside the fabric and ran a warm hand across my bare skin, sending fireworks to explode through my chest. My heart pummeled against my rib cage as my fingers tangled in his hair. Sweet, sweet adrenaline coursed through me, igniting every nerve ending in my body in a warm tingle.

"More," I moaned between his kisses as his hand roamed over my breast.

I hadn't even realized I'd said anything until his weight lifted off of me and he resituated himself to lie beside me on the bed. His lips stayed on mine, but his hand left my breast and trailed downward, running further beneath the sheets. His fingers stopped at my waistband.

No, don't stop!

I curled my fingers deeper into his hair and bit his lower lip, letting him know he was welcome. His hands slipped beneath the fabric. I let out a wavered breath. He paused for a moment, until I protested by deepening our kiss and digging my nails into his shoulder. He responded by kissing me back with equal passion. Then he slid his fingers further down my body until he was touching me *there*. My back arched, and a deep breath passed my lips.

His fingers moved across me in ways I'd never experienced before. The motion sent a fire to build up inside of me, until I was biting his shoulder just to keep the moans from escaping. And then that fire exploded, rushing through me like a blessing from the gods.

Venn pulled the covers up to my chin and wrapped me in his arms. I lay beside him feeling weightless. I couldn't think straight. He placed a kiss on the back of my neck.

"Good night," he whispered.

"What about you?" I mumbled.

"Shh…" he replied softly. "Don't worry about me. We'll have plenty of other chances."

Plenty of other chances. I liked the sound of a future together.

I took a deep breath, inhaling his scent and melting into his chest, before I dozed off into a peaceful slumber.

13

I stared into Venn's eyes—only, the face wasn't his. Still, I recognized him just the same. My fingers reached out to wrap in his. My skin was darker than normal, but only by a shade or two. His was paler than mine, in stark contrast to his usual midnight-dark skin. He dressed in clothing that didn't look to fit this century, and we stood in a thick forest where no one else could hear us. Somehow, I knew our home lay just on the other side of the trees.

"I think it's a good idea," he said, taking my hands in his. "But we don't have to do this, Abigail."

"Yes, we do, Charles," I countered. I barely recognized my own accent. "It's the only way to save everyone."

He dropped my hands and pulled me into an embrace. I leaned into him and rested my head on his shoulder.

"You know what this means, don't you?" I whispered. "If we do this, we will never stop hunting down the vampires."

"I know," he replied, "and I'm okay with that."

"Our lives will never be the same," I said.

"No, they won't," he agreed, "but our lives already changed months ago when they killed our daughters. No one should have to *go through what we went through. We'll rid the world of vampires if it's the last thing we do."*

"Get up!"

I startled awake, my heart thumping wildly against my chest. "Jesus Christ, Fiona!"

She bounced on her knees at the foot of the bed, shaking the springs all the way up by my head. Venn rolled away from me and rubbed the sleep from his eyes. Cool air that tasted a lot like disappointment rushed between us.

I forced my eyes open and glanced to the digital clock on the nightstand. "It's five a.m.!"

Fiona climbed off the bed. "I know, but we have to be at the airport in less than an hour. So, chop-chop."

I sighed and leaned my head back on the pillow as Fiona hurried out of the room, leaving Venn and me alone. My heart was still racing.

"Are you okay?" Venn reached out to touch my shoulder. Although his skin only made contact with my robe, my shoulder heated beneath his touch.

I raked my fingers through my hair and stared blankly up at the ceiling. "Yeah, I'm fine. I just… I think I had a vision."

Venn propped himself on his elbow, immediately alert. "A vision?"

"A vision, or a memory or something." My gaze met his. "It was us, Venn. In our past life."

The worried look on his face vanished. Intrigue replaced it. "Really?"

I nodded. "We were young and living in Europe. It was the mid-1700s. We had three daughters."

Venn opened his mouth to speak, but I cut him off.

"Don't ask me how I know all the details. I just remember."

He smiled. "We really had three girls?"

I nodded, but I knew the sadness was written all over my face. Venn's expression fell.

"They were the reason we started hunting vampires," I explained. "I mean, when we were Abigail and Charles. The vampires..."

My throat closed up. I knew the girls weren't *my* daughters, not in this life, but my heart still broke for them. A muscle fluttered in Venn's jaw.

I squeezed my eyes closed and shook my head, as if trying to rid myself of the memory. "We were discussing our options. You wanted me—Abigail—to perform the spell, the one that turned you into a shifter. You wanted to save everyone else from the vampires."

It didn't surprise me that Charles sounded so much like the Venn I knew.

Venn shifted beside me and pulled me close to his chest. He didn't say anything as he placed a gentle kiss on my forehead. Warmth spread across my skin, calming me.

I drew away. "That's all I remember."

"That's okay," Venn said gently. The look in his eyes told me he meant it. "The fact that you remembered anything at all from your previous life is amazing."

I lifted the corner of my lips into a smile. "Thanks."

Fiona stuck her head back in the room. "Come on, you guys. Breakfast will be here soon. You don't want Ryland to eat all your food, do you?"

She left the room again, and Venn and I exchanged an amused glance.

He groaned and rolled away from me, the muscles in his

back rippling as he pushed himself up. "She's right. Ryland eats like a bear."

I stifled a laugh.

Venn rolled his eyes as he pulled a shirt on over his head. "Don't laugh at me. That was a cheap joke."

"What?" I asked innocently as I pushed myself up to sit on the edge of the bed. "I'm not allowed to find you funny?"

Venn pressed his lips together, like he was thinking hard. "I guess, if that's the kind of humor that entertains you. But in that case, we need to get you out more."

I crawled across the bed and rose to my knees beside him. My hands tangled in his shirt as I tugged on him, encouraging him to come back to bed with me. "I'd rather stay in."

Venn caved to my invite and parted his lips. My tongue grazed across his lower lip as his hands roamed my backside. Every nerve in my body came to life.

He drew away and took a deep breath. "Fiona was serious, you know. If we aren't out there by the time breakfast arrives, we won't get any."

I stuck my lower lip out in a mock pout. "Fine, but we need to make up all the cuddles we missed from being woken up so early."

Venn's eyes sparkled. "We'll have plenty of time for that on our flight."

Reluctantly, I dragged myself out of bed. Venn grabbed his shoes and left the room, closing the door behind him. I tugged at the tie on my robe and let the fabric fall to the floor.

Suddenly, I felt *extremely* exposed. The hairs on the back of my neck stood as if the air conditioning was blowing directly on me, but the vent was all the way across the room and it hadn't been turned on all night. I quickly scooped up the robe from the floor and held it close to my chest while I glanced around the room. The door was securely closed, and the curtains were drawn. I could hear everyone else talking out in the main room.

And still, something didn't feel right—as if someone was watching me.

I shook off the feeling and quickly pulled on my clothes. By the time I'd laced up my boots and tossed my hair into a ponytail with Fiona's brush and one of the hair ties she'd left lying on the dresser, the anxiety rushing through my veins had waned, but the strangeness of the sensation lingered. I exited the room, running my fingers through my hair, to see that everyone was seated around the dining table with plates of food in front of them. I slid into the chair beside Venn, my eyes darting around the room the whole time.

"You look worried," Sondra observed as she took a bite of pancake.

"No," I lied, picking up my fork. "I was just wondering about that protection charm you got from Genevieve."

Way to be subtle.

"What was it for?" I asked.

"This?" Sondra held up the small black bag from where it hung off her neck.

I took a bite of egg and nodded.

"It's a blend of herbs that's supposed to protect us from other magic," Sondra admitted.

"Does it work?" I asked hopefully. Maybe it was just my imagination getting to me.

"It should."

"And what if it didn't work?" I asked. "Matias has the locket. He could be tracking us."

I hated putting my fears out there in the open, but it was a very real possibility.

"Why would he track us?" Ryland cut in. "He's unaware we know about The Wise Owl, isn't he?"

"Well, those guys at Amalia's didn't attack us for no reason," I pointed out.

Ryland opened his mouth to say more, but Sondra cut him off.

"You're right," she said. "That's why we have to get on an early flight and follow Genevieve's coordinates."

"Do we know the coordinates yet?" Teagan asked.

"No," Sondra answered with a shake of her head. "She'll send the coordinates once we land."

Teagan's eyebrows rose. "Where are we going, exactly?"

Sondra swallowed another bite of food. "We won't know until we get to the airport. The reason Genevieve hasn't told us where we're going yet is in case Matias *is* watching us."

"And you trust her?" Ryland asked skeptically.

"Yes," Sondra said. "On this, I do. As long as we make it there before Matias does, everything should work out."

"*Will* we make it there before him?" Venn asked, sounding worried.

"I don't see how he would make it ahead of us," Sondra replied. "Don't worry. We're going to get this thing and destroy it. We'll figure out the rest from there. Any other questions?" Her eyes scanned the table.

Fiona's hand shot into the air. "Yeah, um… can I have a window seat?"

The car Genevieve provided was stocked with everything we needed for the plane ride: travel snacks, magazines for entertainment, and our plane tickets. What surprised me, though, was the sight of my I.D. sitting in the folder with the plane tickets.

I gasped and grabbed it, flipping it around in my hands to make sure it was real. How did it get there?

Inside the folder, a yellow sticky note read, *I figured you'd need this. The rest of your belongings are at my house for when you return. Genevieve.*

Genevieve must've gone to my apartment and taken the bag I'd packed before I left. I was relieved to know my stuff was safe, even though it was just my phone, my spell journal, and a few pairs of clothes. At least it meant my sketchy land-lord didn't have his grubby hands on my stuff.

Almost an hour after we arrived at the airport, we boarded a plane to Nashville.

Fiona inhaled a sharp breath when she saw our destination. "Mammoth Caves," she whispered. "That must be where we're going."

She was the first from our group on the plane. She quickly found our row and settled in by the window, staring out it in wonder even though we hadn't even left the terminal. I sat beside her in the middle seat. Venn placed his bag in the over-head bin before sliding into the seat beside me.

I eyed Fiona curiously. "Have you ever flown before?"

She couldn't tear her gaze off the window. "No, I haven't. If Sondra ever has to travel for business, she always takes Ryland with her."

I glanced to Ryland, who was trying to find enough leg room to rest his feet. He was far too big for the plane and had to spread his legs so his knees didn't touch the back of the seat in front of him. I could see why Sondra took him along. He was a full security team shoved into one body.

"And you, Venn?" I asked. He threw a nervous glance at the window. "Have you ever flown before?"

"I—I did once," he said hesitantly. "When I was a kid, my family flew to California for my cousin's wedding."

"Me, too," I told him. "My family took a vacation to Florida when I was eight. I loved it."

Fiona leaned over and whispered, "Venn hates it."

My shocked gaze snapped in his direction. "You're afraid of flying?"

He nodded, and his hands tightened around his armrests as the plane began to roll away from the terminal. I felt bad for him. I couldn't imagine being afraid of flying. Granted, when I flew it typically wasn't in an airplane, and I usually had the wind whipping through my feathers to add to the thrill, but still…

"It's okay, Venn," I said lightly as I rested a hand on his. "I live for flying. I wouldn't let anything happen to you."

A ghost of a smile touched his lips. "Thanks."

When we reached the runway, his hand tightened around mine. He closed his eyes and took a deep breath as we picked up speed. I knew when the plane's wheels left the ground because my stomach flipped in my abdomen. Venn squeezed my fingers so tightly he could've crushed bone.

Beside me, Fiona gasped as the earth dropped out from beneath us. "Oh, wow! It's so pretty from up here. Venn, look!"

Venn didn't open his eyes. Ryland muttered something under his breath. I didn't catch it, but I figured it was some sort of insult. Teagan slugged him in the arm. My gaze darted to Sondra across the aisle, wondering what I should do to help Venn.

"There's no shame in being scared," Sondra said simply.

"Most people see fear as a weakness, but it's how you use fear that matters."

This woman was freaking wise. I wanted to be her someday.

"What do you mean?" I asked, intrigued.

She leaned on her armrest and stuck her head into the aisle. "Fear is important to self-preservation. There's such thing as too much fear, so much that it keeps you from truly living. But if you fear nothing, you will almost certainly get yourself killed. A healthy amount of fear is a good thing. Venn's learned that and knows how to handle it."

He nodded, his eyes still closed. "She's right. I'll be fine. I just need a minute."

"I'm scared of things most people aren't, too," Fiona chimed in. "Vampires, for one."

I looked at her in disbelief. "You are not." I didn't want to say too much with other passengers around, but Fiona freaking slayed the bastards.

"No, really," she insisted. "I do what I have to do, but honestly, I've just been lucky. Hey, Ryland, remember that time when you threw up and that vamp slipped in it while he was coming after me? If Ryland hadn't been sick, I don't know if I'd be here today."

I briefly wondered why we were talking about vampires out in the open like this. Most people didn't take kindly to our vampire-slaying hobbies, considering the bloodsuckers still had rights. Then I caught a glimpse of Venn's face and saw that his expression had relaxed. Fiona was talking to distract him.

"I'm scared of the dumbest things, too," I joined in.

"Really?" Teagan's brows shot up from across the aisle. "Rae? Scared? No way."

"Yes way," I said with a laugh. "I'm scared of…"

What was I scared of? Certainly not vampires. I was scared of being alone again, of going back to my old life where I had no friends, no family. But this wasn't the kind of conversation that warranted diving that deep. I was supposed to be making Venn feel better.

"Maggots," I settled with.

"Maggots?" Teagan laughed.

"They're gross!" I argued. "I just don't want them touching me. When I was little, my sister and I found a dead mouse at the park by our house. It was full of maggots. She told me it was the mouse's insides coming to life and that he was going to become a zombie mouse. I ran home screaming."

Fiona snickered from beside me. The memory churned my insides. When Venn peeled his eyes open, everything I'd just said was so totally worth it.

He smirked. "And you believed her?"

I shrugged, holding back a laugh. "Of course I did. I was, like, five. Anything's possible when you're five."

"True," he agreed, relaxing his hands on the armrest. "I used to believe my toys came to life at night."

"I did, too," I giggled. "*Toy Story* was my favorite movie. I thought it was real."

Venn laughed. "I once apologized to a toy soldier because I stepped on him. For the longest time, I thought he'd died and the other soldiers had buried him, because I couldn't find him after that. I eventually found him in my brother's room months later."

"You guys had it easy," Fiona teased. "Ryland convinced me my dolls were evil. I couldn't sleep for weeks until Mom and Dad locked my dolls up in their closet. I only played with puzzles for, like, six months before I got a stuffed bear for my birthday." Fiona shot Ryland daggers.

Ryland looked up from the game he was playing on the screen in front of him. "Hey, I said I was sorry, like, a million times."

"Only because Mom and Dad made you," she shot back with a laugh.

I grinned. "So, what I'm hearing is that Ryland's always been a jerk."

Fiona wrinkled her nose. "Mostly. But he can be sweet sometimes."

"*Sometimes?*" Ryland repeated. "I'm a freaking jar of strawberry jam. I'm as sweet as they come."

"Oh, honey." Teagan patted his leg. "You're strawberry jam if they forgot to add the sugar."

Sondra chose that moment to take a swig from her water bottle. She nearly choked as she tried to keep from spraying her water all over the seat in front of her. She coughed to compose herself. "I've never heard anyone speak such truth before." She screwed the cap back on and high-fived Teagan.

The plane ride wasn't long, but Venn and I passed the time by tossing peanuts into the air and trying to catch them in our mouths.

I caught the first three, but the forth landed on the side of my cheek and shot out into the middle of the aisle. Venn leaned over and grabbed it. I opened my mouth, and he took aim. It hit me square on the end of the nose.

"Excuse me," a voice snapped. A steward with a bald patch stopped in the aisle next to our seats. He gazed down at us with judgement in his eyes. "But I'm going to have to ask you to stop."

Venn and I exchanged a guilty glance.

I cleared my throat. "Yes, sir. We're sorry."

I held back my laugh, clearly not meaning it.

The steward nodded and turned from us, his nose held high. I threw a peanut at the back of the guy's head as he walked away. Fiona and Venn both broke out into a fit of laughter.

Eventually, I lay my head against Venn's shoulder and stared out the window at the rising sun. I was enjoying the flight so much that I nearly forgot where we were headed until we landed.

"The car's this way," Sondra said with confidence once we stepped off the plane.

We followed her through the airport until we came to a parking garage.

Sondra stopped beside a silver minivan and glanced at her phone. "This is it. Genevieve says the keys are in the glovebox and there are supplies for us in the back."

Sondra headed to the driver's side door and opened it. She poked her head inside the van and came out holding a white slip of paper. She smiled and turned the paper to us. "Genevieve says good luck."

"Should we check out what she left us?" Ryland suggested, popping open the back hatch.

"Ooh. Fancy," Fiona said when she saw the six backpacks piled up behind the back seat.

Venn reached for the red one on top and unzipped the main pocket. "Looks like Genevieve thought of everything. Water, headlamps, food, first-aid kit, rope... do you think we'll need rope?"

Sondra shrugged. "We might. I don't know what to expect. We have to prepare for anything."

"Hell yes!" Teagan exclaimed, glancing into a black backpack she'd pulled off the top. She looked up with a wide smile on her face. "Genevieve scored me some throwing knives. I'm going to have to rethink my feelings on this lady."

"You can go through your bags in the car. We should get going," Sondra suggested. "I don't want to waste any time."

"How far is the drive?" I asked.

Sondra glanced down at her phone. "It looks like it'll take about two hours. I can get us there in one and a half." She smiled mischievously.

My brows shot up. "I didn't know you were a speed demon. I like it."

Teagan let out a light laugh while she climbed into the van. "You say that now."

Fiona rolled her eyes and opened the passenger-side door. "Because you're a *much* better driver."

"I never claimed that," Teagan laughed before turning her attention to Ryland. "Hey, babe. You wanna sit in the back by me? We can make out like lovesick teenagers."

Ryland's eyes lit up, and he eagerly climbed in and jumped over the seat to sit next to her.

Teagan held up her hands in surrender. "Jeez. I was joking."

"So, you don't want to make out with me?" Ryland leaned over her and stuck his tongue out, threatening to lick her with it.

I stifled a laugh while I slid into the middle seat. Venn sat beside me and closed the door behind us.

"Ew!" Teagan complained, placing a hand on Ryland's chest. "Get that thing away from me."

I knew now wasn't the time to be joking around and laughing, but I couldn't help but enjoy the moment. I'd become so serious over the past few years that I almost forgot there were still things worth laughing over. *And things worth loving*, I thought as my gaze roamed over Venn.

He didn't notice my eyes on him as he draped his arm around my shoulder and settled in for the long car ride. For just a few more hours, I would enjoy the warmth of Venn's embrace and the glorious sound of my new family bickering with each other.

Then it was down into the cold, damp cave, where anything could happen.

14

True to her word, Sondra pulled off a deserted road into a narrow gravel driveway an hour and a half later. The forest was thick around us, and the sun was playing peek-a-boo behind the clouds. Something about the wilderness made me feel free, like I could run for miles or fly high in the sky. Ahead, the trees parted to give way to a clearing where a small cabin sat. It looked old but well taken care of. There were no signs of human life on the property.

"Genevieve said we should park here off the main road," Sondra explained as she slowed the van to a stop. "Technically, we're trespassing, but it's a vacation home that no one's using right now, so we should be fine."

"How far away are the caves?" Venn asked.

"If Genevieve's coordinates are correct, it looks like we have a good three-mile hike ahead of us," Sondra said. "But she says the entrance isn't going to be easy to find, so we're going to have to keep a close eye out for it."

Sondra parked, and we all piled out of the vehicle and strapped our day packs to our backs.

"How are you doing?" Venn whispered under his breath as we entered lush green forest behind everyone else.

"I'm fine. Why?" It sounded like a lie, even to my ears, though I didn't know why. I hadn't realized I was lying.

"Because your sister is still out there," Venn answered. "I can see it in your eyes every now and then that you worry about her."

"I do," I agreed as I stepped around a thick tree and over underbrush. I slowed my pace to put distance between us and the rest of the group. I lowered my voice so only Venn could hear. "I should've gone after her years ago, but I didn't know where to start. I was hopeless. I think that's part of why I started killing vampires—because it gave me hope that the world might be a better place without them."

Venn cocked his head like he agreed with me.

"I miss her so much," I whispered.

"I know," Venn said. "As soon as we're done here, we're going after her. I promise."

I shot him a light smile. "I really appreciate that."

The longer we walked in silence, the more I thought about Jenna. My gut twisted as guilt assaulted me.

She can hold out another day, I told myself, but I wasn't an easy person to convince.

The fact was, thinking about Jenna was sending my anxiety into overdrive. There was nothing I could do right now for her out in the wilderness, and I knew I might need to access magic for whatever lay ahead. So, despite the guilt tearing through me, I pushed her from my mind. *Temporarily,* I told myself.

I took a deep breath and released the tension in my fists on the exhale. I focused on the calming sound of the wind rushing through the trees... until the wind began to pick up. A chill traveled down my spine. The sky began to darken, and the temperature seemed to drop a few degrees within a matter of minutes. Something in the air tasted different, but I couldn't pinpoint what. I hadn't even realized the air normally *had* a taste. I just knew something wasn't quite right.

"It looks like it might rain," Ryland said, glancing up at the sky. "How close are we?"

Sondra stepped around a tree. "Not far. Keep an eye out."

Fiona scanned the landscape. A short hill rose ahead of us, but other than that, the forest was fairly flat. "I don't see how we're going to find a cave around here."

"It could look like anything," Sondra said. "It might just be a hole in the ground."

Fiona's eyes darted to her feet in horror, as if wondering whether or not we were going to fall straight into a cavern.

A familiar tingle spread across my skin, raising the hairs on my arms. I might've written it off as static electricity in the air from the incoming storm if I hadn't been acutely tuned to my magical sense.

"I feel something," I announced.

"I do, too," Sondra agreed. "There's magic up ahead. We're getting close."

As we crested the hill, the energy sizzling across my skin intensified. The hill stopped abruptly at a rocky wall at least ten feet high. We stood at the top of it, overlooking the rest of the forest.

"It's here," I said confidently, though I couldn't tell exactly how I knew. Somehow, I could just *feel* an enchantment in the air.

"What are we waiting for?" Teagan asked. "Let's check it out."

Ryland walked to the edge of the short cliff and jumped

straight down. Fiona inhaled a sharp breath, but he landed just fine at the bottom.

Show off.

"You okay?" Sondra called to him.

He better be, considering the guy was big enough to practically reach up his arms and touch our toes.

"Fine," Ryland said. "Are you coming or what?"

Teagan backed away from the edge. "I'll take the easy way down. I don't plan on breaking any bones today."

"Oh, come on, babe." Ryland held his arms out. "I'll catch you."

Teagan shot him the stink eye, like she didn't believe him.

"Catch me!" Fiona said quickly.

She bent her knees, and a look of horror crossed Ryland's face. She gave a small hop into the air but only came off the ground a few inches.

"You're so gullible," Fiona said with a laugh. She turned away from Ryland and followed Sondra down the side of the hill. "You should've seen your face."

The rest of us took the gentle slope down the lowest corner of the rock wall and climbed down easily. As soon as we reached level ground, I spotted an opening in the rock. It wasn't very big, only about the size of the window back in my apartment. But it sloped downward and stretched so far back into the hillside that all I saw was pitch-black darkness. The magical energy I'd felt earlier was stronger than ever.

I stood in front of the mouth of the cave and placed my hands on my hips, peering inside. Ryland's ass was going to get stuck in there. I was sure of it.

"So... who wants to crawl into the creepy tunnel of doom first?" I asked.

"I'd go first," Fiona offered, "but we have to find the creepy tunnel of doom first. Feel anything else?"

I furrowed my brow as she scanned the forest, totally oblivious to the cave mouth I stood in front of. "Yeah. It's called using my eyes."

"What?" Fiona asked, like I wasn't making any sense.

That's when I noticed everyone's eyes still roaming the rock face. Venn stared out into the trees, as if he might find the mouth of the cave a hundred yards out. Sondra was the only one who seemed to notice the opening.

"They can't see it?" I asked her.

She stepped forward and glanced into the cave. "Apparently not. You feel that magic emanating off the rock face?"

I nodded.

"The rock must be enchanted to hide the cavern," she theorized.

Teagan placed her hands on her hips. "What are you talking about?"

I ignored her and kept my attention on Sondra. "Why can we see it when they can't?"

Sondra thought about it for a beat. "The artifact was made for witches, by witches. The coven that hid it must've enchanted the entrance so that only a witch could find it. That must be why this cavern has remained undiscovered all these years."

"So, if we're the only ones who can see it, are we the only ones who can enter?" I asked.

Sondra shrugged. "Genevieve didn't say anything about an enchanted entrance. From here on out, we're on our own."

Well, shit. That meant *I* was going down the creepy tunnel of doom first. *Bring it on.*

"Now's not the time for games," Ryland warned. "Are you two being serious?"

"Yes," I answered. "You really can't see this?" I gestured to the cave entrance.

Venn stepped forward and ran his hands along the stone, eyeing it in wonder. "That's so weird. To us, it's just a flat rockface."

His hands ran flat across the opening of the cave, as if he were a mime. I wondered what it would look like to them if I entered it. Would I just disappear into the rock like a ghost?

"Let's see what happens if I go inside," I offered.

Venn stepped aside to give me room. I ducked my head and leaned forward, but before I could get my hands on the edge of the opening, the top of my head slammed into something solid. I recoiled, rubbing the area of impact and cursing under my breath. Ryland burst into a fit of laughter behind me. Teagan swatted at him, but she too was stifling a laugh.

"Very funny," I snarled once the curses died down. "I'm not making this shit up. There's a cave right here! It's just…"

I stretched my hand out. My fingers met a cold, hard material I couldn't see.

"Rock?" Ryland finished for me with a raised eyebrow.

Fiona crossed her arms and glared at him. "Well, *I* believe her."

"I didn't say I didn't believe her!" Ryland rebutted.

"Can you guys just chill for a minute?" Sondra insisted. "I need to think."

Everyone went silent as Sondra ran her hand over the invisible rock face and inspected the enchanted cave opening.

After what felt like several minutes, I dared to break the silence. "Didn't Amalia say that only the witch who created a spell can break it?"

"Usually, if the spell is strong enough," Sondra answered without looking up at me. She was on her knees now, inspecting the rock. "But this enchantment was meant to be broken."

"How do we break it?" Teagan asked.

"Genevieve should've known about this," Venn said with uncertainty in his eyes. "She didn't mention anything to you?"

Sondra tilted her head to look at the underside of the rocks jutting out from the wall. "No, which means there must be a clue around here somewhere."

Fiona joined Sondra on her knees to inspect the rock. She shot the rest of us a look of disapproval. "What are you all waiting for?"

Before we had a chance to join in, Sondra spoke. "Hold on. I found something."

Sondra gazed into the cave and stared at something on the rock ceiling. I squeezed in beside her to take a look. Beyond the invisible wall, a string of words had been engraved into the stone.

"*Witches rise, and witches fall, but a heart that's pure and clean will enter with revelare, three tears, and smoke of evergreen,*" Sondra recited. She stood and dusted off her knees. "This is our way in."

Confusion crossed Ryland's face. "What does it mean? *A heart that's pure and clean?* So, we need a virgin witch to get us through? Where are we going to find one of those?"

I glared at him and placed a hand on my hip. "Really? You're just going to assume I'm *not* a virgin witch?"

"Ryland," Teagan scolded.

"I was just—"

"We don't need a virgin," Sondra cut him off.

Ryland rose his eyebrows. "I suppose you're going to cast the spell? Your heart's not exactly pure and clean."

Sondra scowled at him. "I've made my amends, and you know that. Now, would you stop it and go find some pine needles?"

"Pine needles?" Ryland asked in confusion.

"Yes," Sondra emphasized. "Did you miss the part about *smoke of evergreen*, or were you too focused on sacrificing a virgin?"

Ryland held his hands up in surrender. "I heard it. I just don't know where I'm supposed to find pine needles. This isn't exactly a coniferous forest."

Teagan spun around and grabbed Ryland's huge bicep. "Come on. It's the least we can do to help."

Sondra shook her head and turned back to the cave opening once Ryland and Teagan walked away. "Cousins. I tell ya."

"Hey," Fiona dragged out in mock offense.

"Relax, Fiona. You're practically my sister," Sondra said with a smile.

"Aww…" Fiona blinked rapidly and fanned her face like she was touched.

"Keep that up," Venn encouraged. "We're going to need three of those tears."

Fiona smiled. "Always happy to help."

I shifted my weight between my feet. "So, we have the evergreen and the tears. What about that first part? *Revelare?*"

"That's the incantation," Sondra explained. "So once we have the pine needles, we should be able to get through. It's actually a really simple spell."

"Should we go help look—?"

I was cut off by the sound of a twig breaking in the

distance. I whirled around, expecting to see Ryland and Teagan on their way back, but the forest was empty. Chills immediately danced up and down my arms, but I quickly realized it was just the cool breeze from the storm rolling in.

Just as I thought it, the first of the heavy raindrops fell. One splattered against the tip of my nose while another hit the back of my hand. I glanced up to the sky just as the clouds opened and it began pouring.

Fiona ducked and pulled her backpack up over her head. Within seconds, my hair was sticking to my face, and my shoulders were soaked. I instinctively hugged the edge of the rock, hoping the cliff would provide some relief from the rain, but there wasn't an overhang to protect us from the downpour.

I cursed under my breath. "How are we going to get smoke in this kind of weather? And what if Ryland and Teagan get lost?"

Venn was quick to act and pulled a small tarp out of his bag. He unfolded it and draped it over the two of us.

"Come on." He gestured for Sondra and Fiona to join us.

The tarp was barely big enough to cover the four of us, and we had to hold on to the corners tightly to make sure the wind whipping by us wouldn't steal it away.

"What do we do?" Fiona yelled to be heard over the strong wind. "Should we go looking for them?"

"There they are!" Sondra pointed, her finger getting wet beneath the rain.

Two shadows sprinted forward. I blinked away the water from my eyes and pushed my wet hair from my face. Teagan came to a halt in front of us and quickly threw the remaining corner of the tarp over her head. Ryland stood in the rain, using his backpack as an umbrella. It was so small compared to his large frame that it looked more like he was trying to keep dry with a soggy piece of bread.

"Here!" Teagan shoved a pile of pine needles and twigs into Sondra's hand. "Sorry they're wet."

"That's fine," Sondra said in a rush. She placed the pine needles on the small piece of rock that stuck out just beneath the cave opening.

Venn stretched his arm around me to hold the tarp over Sondra's workstation. My breath caught in my chest as his arm brushed against the side of my head.

"Who has tears for me?" Sondra asked.

"Working on them," Fiona said. Her lips turned down, and her eyes sparkled like a puppy dog's. She squeezed her eyes shut, trying to force the tears.

"Dead puppies," Ryland blurted.

"That's just cruel," Teagan snapped at him.

"You need tears," Ryland said. "I'm just trying to help."

"Babe—" Teagan started to scold, but Fiona cut her off.

"No, it's fine. The more horrible things he throws at me, the better chance I have of crying." Fiona blinked, forcing the tears out. Water dripped down her face, but I was ninety-nine percent sure that those were rain droplets and not tears. We were going to have to break someone's foot if we wanted tears on demand.

I could cry, I thought to myself. I mean, I hated crying, but I wasn't so emotionally detached that I couldn't shed a tear.

"Think of Mom and Dad," Ryland encouraged.

I knew the words were for Fiona, but I let my thoughts drift to my own parents. For the first time in what felt like years, I dropped my emotional walls and recalled the memories I'd pushed away for so long. My chest tightened as I thought back to my mother's soft smile and the way my dad's scruffy beard felt across my face when he kissed my cheek. I could still smell the scent of my mother's signature Summer Sunshine shampoo. I thought of the time she held me in her arms while I cried one night when I was twelve, the day Wendy Bolton punched me in the face for flirting with the guy she liked. I remembered the proud look in my dad's eyes the next day when he was teaching me how to defend myself. I'd knocked him off his feet on my third try. I remembered how Jenna had offered to kick Wendy's ass herself if she ever touched me again.

God, I missed my family. We weren't always perfect, but we always had each other's backs.

And now they're gone.

The words echoed in my mind. My parents were gone forever. And Jenna... who knew?

My cheeks heated. Tears welled in my eyes and poured over the lids. I quickly leaned over the pine needle pile and squeezed my eyes shut to let the tears fall. When satisfied that at least three tears had been added to the pile, I pulled away and wiped the rest from my cheeks. I opened my eyes to see everyone staring at me in shock.

"What?" I shrugged. "I have feelings, you know."

Sondra shot me a somber look, then pulled her attention away from me and to the pine needles. Venn wasn't as quick to dismiss my display. He wrapped his free arm around my shoulder and pressed his cheek to the top of my head. He didn't say anything, but he didn't have to. Already, I felt warmer, and the weight on my chest began to ease beneath his embrace.

"Let's speed it up," Ryland pressed. "I'm soaked."

Sondra muttered an incantation I recognized under her breath, and the wet pine needles ignited.

"Revelare," she said as the fire quickly ate away at the needles and smoke rose into the air.

The smoke instantly changed directions, swooping into the cave mouth as if it'd been sucked into a vacuum. Everyone but Sondra and me drew a collective breath. I knew they could now see the deep, dark hole in the side of the rock.

"I'll go in first and make sure it's safe," Sondra said hastily, rising to her feet. "Ryland, you go last and make sure everyone gets through okay."

"I will," he agreed, dropping the childish demeanor from earlier. Clearly, he knew things were about to get serious.

Fiona followed behind Sondra, and I went in after her. I crawled in on my hands and knees, relieved that it was dry. The entrance wasn't much bigger than the covered slide at my old elementary school, and it sloped down at a similar angle. Ahead of me, Sondra's light cast shadows across the tunnel. Too bad I hadn't grabbed my headlamp. It felt like I was crawling into the belly of a beast that wanted nothing more than to eat me alive.

Good thing I had plenty of experience slaying monsters.

15

The tunnel widened, giving way to a cavern I could stand in. The space wasn't much bigger than the bathroom back in the suite we'd stayed in, but the ceiling was at least four feet higher. Under the light of Sondra's headlamp, I could see that three tunnels split off from the room in different directions.

I stepped away from the tunnel we came through to give everyone else room to stand. I swung my backpack off my shoulder and set it on a damp rocky ledge along the wall of the cave. I found a headlamp in the front pocket and strapped it to my forehead.

"This one's a dead end," Fiona announced as she peeked into one of the tunnels.

I stepped toward the opposite one and shone my light down it. All I saw was a rocky wall and muddy floor.

"This one, too," I said.

Venn emerged from the tunnel and stood, glancing around the cave in wonder.

"This one goes forward," Sondra said, gesturing the last tunnel. "It must be this way."

Teagan and Ryland reached the cavern.

"Can we maybe dry off?" Ryland asked, gesturing to his soaking clothes.

"We don't need Sondra using any more magic than she has to," Venn objected.

Ryland considered his words for a moment. "True. I suppose I'll survive."

"You better," Fiona said. "I'm not losing my brother in here."

Ryland cracked a smile, though I didn't think he realized anyone noticed.

"Aw, isn't that sweet?" Teagan feigned. "Let's get going."

We started down the only tunnel that led anywhere. It was cramped at first, barely allowing enough room for my hips and shoulders to squeeze through. We went single-file. Ryland had to go sideways so that his shoulders would fit. It felt like the walls were squeezing in on us. The farther we went, the less I felt like I could breathe. All I heard were the footsteps and the sound of everyone else's breathing around me.

After a good five minutes in the Suffocation Tunnel, the ceiling gradually dropped, but the walls of the cave widened until we could walk side-by-side. We came to a room that was bigger than the last one, but it appeared as if we'd hit a dead end. That was, until our lights passed across the five-foot-wide hole in the ground.

Sondra approached the pit cautiously and glanced inside. She sighed. "I'd get us all down there with telekinesis, but that's going to take too much out of me. I'd pass out by the time we were done. It looks like that rope Genevieve gave us is going to come in handy."

Fiona held on to Sondra for support and peeked over the edge. "Who wants to drop forty feet to their death first?"

Venn and I reached the rocky ledge and glanced inside the pit. Rock outlined the hole like an old-time well for about ten feet before a wide cavity opened below us. It looked like an acrophobic person's worst nightmare.

"No one's scared of heights, are they?" I asked.

Ryland took a look, shining his headlamp into the hole. "Pfft. That's easy. I could jump that far."

"Then I guess you're going first," Teagan challenged him.

Ryland stepped back from the edge. "Hell no."

"We'll go one at a time," Sondra cut in, taking charge. "Venn, you had the rope in your bag, didn't you?"

"Yeah." Venn swung his bag off his shoulder and pulled open the main zipper.

"How are we going to do this?" Fiona asked. "There's nothing around here to safely secure the rope to. We can't just leave someone behind."

"I'll go last," I offered. "I can fly, so I don't need the rope anyway. And you all know I'm strong enough to lower you down."

Ryland shrugged. "Good enough for me. I trust her."

"Then you're up first," Venn said with a smile as he tossed one end of the black rope into the pit. I heard it hit the bottom with a soft *thwack*.

"I'll assist as much as I can," Sondra offered.

"Nah, I got this," Ryland declined. "Don't tire yourself out. We don't know how much energy you might need later."

Venn, Teagan, and Fiona helped me hold the rope as

Ryland climbed down. Sondra slid down the rope next, then Teagan.

"What's down there?" Venn called.

"It's a big cavern," Ryland replied. "About the size of our house. There's only one tunnel leading out, but we're going to have to climb. It's about fifteen feet off the ground."

"You go next," Fiona said to Venn. "I'm the lightest, so I'll go last. That way I can help Rae hold you up."

Venn nodded in agreement. "Just don't drop me."

"Then don't doubt us," I teased lightheartedly. "Or we just might."

"Would you now?" He smirked back at me.

"No," I admitted, "but we could."

"Stop batting your eyes at each other, and let's go," Ryland called up to us. "We're losing daylight here."

Fiona shook her head as she grabbed the rope and braced herself. "My brother's an idiot."

"We know," Venn agreed with a light laugh.

I planted my feet firmly on the ground and held on tightly to the rope wrapped halfway around my torso. Venn lay on his stomach and grabbed the rope, shimmying his way down. It vibrated in my hands as he descended. I felt when he touched ground because the weight on the rope vanished, and it went slack again.

Fiona stepped forward cautiously. "So... uh, how do I do this?"

"Lie on your stomach and dangle your feet into the hole," Sondra instructed. "Then grab the rope and plant your feet on the side of the rock to work your way down."

Fiona lay on the ground as she was instructed. "This, uh, doesn't seem safe."

Sondra hadn't heard her. "Once there's no more rock,

you'll lock your feet around the rope and slide the rest of the way down."

"Can you help me just a little?" Fiona shouted. "With telekinesis, I mean?"

"I can assist," Sondra offered, "but don't rely on it completely, okay?"

"Okay," Fiona agreed. "I'm ready!"

Fiona barely tugged on the rope as her weight left the ground. Suddenly, her weight shifted. A collective gasp came from everyone else in the cavern below me. My heart lurched at the sound of rock against rock impacting and echoing off the chamber walls.

"What happened?" I cried. I could still feel Fiona's weight on the rope, so as far as I knew, she was safe, but my heart still hammered as if something had gone terribly wrong.

"It's okay!" Fiona called up to me. "I'm okay. I just dislodged a rock. Not much further to—"

"Shit!" Teagan cried.

"What the—?" Sondra cut off.

Everyone else's voices filled the air as the sound of rushing water met my ears. Fiona screamed, and I felt the rope rushing back and forth.

My stomach bottomed out. "What's going on?"

"Water!" Fiona called up to me. "The whole cavern's filling with water. Sondra, help me! I don't know how much longer I can—"

The rope went slack. The sickening crunch of breaking bone met my ears, and Fiona's shriek echoed throughout the cave.

My heart stopped as I rushed forward and fell to my knees at the side of the hole. "Fiona! Oh my God. What happened?"

Everyone surrounded Fiona, all talking at once so that I

couldn't make out any of their words. They hovered over her so that I couldn't see what had happened. Fiona screamed out in agony.

"Is she okay?" I demanded, though I knew deep down that something had gone terribly wrong.

And it was only going to get worse. In the cavern below me, water rushed across the floor. It touched Venn's shoes, rising quickly.

"I'm sorry!" Sondra cried. "I was distracted by the water. I'm going to fix this, okay? Just lie back. The pain will only last another minute."

Venn turned his gaze up to me as Sondra began muttering an incantation under her breath. I shielded my eyes so I wouldn't be blinded by his headlamp.

"She broke her leg. The cavern's filling with water—and fast," Venn explained.

"We need to go back," Teagan insisted from where she knelt beside Fiona.

"It's just another obstacle—a booby trap," Ryland said. "Someone should take Fiona back to the car. The rest of us can keep going."

"We don't know what lies ahead!" Teagan countered. She shot to her feet and moved aside just far enough that I could see Fiona's leg bent at an odd angle. "What if this whole cavern fills with water and there's no way out through that tunnel over there?"

I was already stripping my backpack off. "I'm coming down!"

I didn't wait for anyone to respond as I dropped my bag and headlamp to the ground and shifted into raven form. Without hesitation, I dove into the cavern and landed beside Fiona. The water was halfway up my shins, and Fiona's body was hovering just inches above it as Sondra continued her incantation. Fiona's screams died down, and her eyes rolled back in her head.

"I can help," I offered. I forced my shaking hands to steady, thinking back to Sondra's lesson on controlling my emotions. It hadn't been much, but it was all I had. "That way you won't drain your energy so fast."

"Okay," Sondra agreed. "But we have to act quickly. She can't feel a thing right now, so we're going to have to set the bone."

"I'll take her back," Teagan offered. "The rest of you are more useful in this cave than I am."

"No, Tea—" Ryland started to protest, but Sondra cut him off.

"We don't have time to argue," she said in a surprisingly calm voice.

You need to stay calm, too, Rachel, I reminded myself. *Now's not the time to freak out. Remember what Genevieve said about resilience. You're going to need it today. So grow a set of lady balls and calm your tits.*

"Teagan will take Fiona back, and the rest of us will continue on," Sondra decided. "Ryland, hold Fiona's leg here. On the count of three—"

The sound of rocks clashing together rumbled above us. The water rising around us rippled. Alarm shot to everyone's faces.

"Did that just sound like—?" I started.

"A cave-in?" Venn's voice rose several pitches.

I cursed. "I'll go check it out. You help Fiona."

I shifted and shot into the air. There was no light to guide me through the tunnel and back to the entrance of the cave, but I could sense where I was by the sound of air coming off my wings and bouncing off the cave walls. The tips of my wings skimmed the edge of the tunnel several times, almost knocking me out of the air, but by some miracle, I managed to stay airborne.

I knew when I'd hit the first cavern because the air moved differently, sounded different. I landed and shifted back to human form, my chest heaving from the exertion. My eyes darted around the pitch-black cavern. There should've been a sliver of light cast through the darkness, even in the midst of the storm, but darkness completely consumed me.

I stepped toward the wall and ran my hands over a rocky ledge. I knew it was the same one I'd set my bag on earlier. Inching further along the wall, I felt my way across the cavern until my hands met nothing but air. It was the opening to the room I'd looked into before, the one that was nothing but a dead end.

Skipping over the dead-end room, I continued along the wall until I thought I was standing in front of the tunnel leading outside. My foot caught a rock, and my ankle twisted under me. I crashed to the ground and caught myself on a sharp rock.

Fear tumbled around in my gut as my fingers blindly roamed over rock after rock. In the quiet, I could just barely make out the sound of wind whistling through the rock. The storm outside raged on, but I would've preferred standing out in a thunderstorm to my new reality.

We were trapped.

I sprinted down the tunnel, back to Venn and the others. When I broke out of the narrow space and into the room with the hole in the ground, my eyes finally found a dull glow from a flashlight. But light wasn't the only thing I found. Fiona lay on her back, and Teagan leaned over her.

"I'm going to need you to shift, Fiona," Teagan demanded. "It's the only way I can carry you back."

"It hurts," Fiona cried, tears streaming down her face.

"Sondra shouldn't have wasted power getting you back up here," I said breathlessly.

"Rae?" Venn called up to me.

"Yeah," I shouted back.

"We need to leave now!" he cried. "There's a tunnel, but—"

I stuck my head over the top of the hole so I could see him. "The main entrance caved in. Teagan and Fiona are going to have to come with us."

Teagan shot to her feet. "What?!"

I whirled toward her. "I'm sorry, but we can't go back the way we came. Our only chance is to go forward."

"How are we going to get Fiona...?" Teagan glanced down at her somberly. She lowered her voice. "Sondra did a pain relief spell, but it's already wearing off. This isn't something you can just heal in a matter of minutes."

"I know," I said.

"We'll stay here—" Teagan started.

"And what if the water rises to this room?" I asked. "There's no other way out. Fiona, you can shift, can't you?"

"Not with a broken leg," she protested. "What if it doesn't heal right?"

Teagan bent beside her and stripped off her backpack. She pulled open the main pocket and began digging the contents out of it. "Your leg will heal fine. Sondra made sure of that. Now, will you please shift and get in the bag? I'll carry you the rest of the way."

I bent to scoop up Teagan's food and supplies, then put them in my bag that still sat beside the hole.

Fiona groaned and shifted into a small fox. She was careful not to put any weight on her leg as Teagan helped her into the backpack and zipped up the sides to secure her in, leaving nothing but her head poking out.

"What's going on up there?" Venn demanded. "I meant it when I said we had to leave now."

I picked up my headlamp from where I'd left it on the ground and adjusted it on my head. "Watch out. We're coming down!"

I glanced into the hole to see the water was high and the coast was clear. Without hesitation, I jumped.

Cold water hit my skin and swallowed me up. My feet touched the cave floor. I bent my knees sand shot myself upward. I sucked in a deep breath when my head broke the surface, and I wiped the water from my eyes. When I opened them, my gaze fell on Venn, who was treading water several feet away from me. Reaching out my arm and kicking my feet, I swam over to him.

"You're okay?" he asked with concern.

I nodded. "I am."

"Tea?" Sondra called up to us.

"Coming!" Teagan shouted. "Hold your breath, Fiona."

Teagan leapt into the hole. Water splashed into my face when she landed. She came up for air a moment later, and Fiona sputtered in the backpack behind her.

"Let's go," Sondra ordered.

I swam behind her. Ahead of us, a tunnel was carved out high in the room. The water had already reached the base of the tunnel and was rising fast.

"This can't be the only way out," I theorized. "This water has to go somewhere."

"The water's enchanted," Sondra replied with certainty. "In fact, the whole cavern is probably enchanted. Can't you feel it?"

Now that she mentioned it, I could feel a tingle of magic if I focused closely.

"So, how do we know this is the tunnel we have to go down?" Ryland asked, making strong strokes through the water.

Sondra's hands curled against the edge of the tunnel, and she pulled herself onto a dry cave floor. She turned to give me a hand. "We don't, but we sure as hell don't have time to figure out if there's another enchanted tunnel around here. The water's rising too fast."

Ryland bent to pull Teagan from the water just as it hit the edge of the tunnel. The cavern we'd just been swimming through looked like a lake. I shivered from the cold. Venn's gaze roamed my body and settled on my goosebumps, but he didn't get a chance to offer me relief from the chill.

"What the—?" Teagan said.

The water rose higher and higher, but it stopped at the opening of the tunnel. It met up with an invisible barrier, as if there were a pane of glass between the tunnel and the lake.

Ryland breathed a sigh of relief. "Thank God. The tunnel's safe."

Sondra didn't take her eyes off the water surface as she stepped away from it. "Let's not make any assumptions. Come on. We don't know how far we have to go."

We hurried down the tunnel, leaving the water behind us. The lights from our headlamps bounced up and down against the rock on either side of us. Ahead, there was nothing but darkness, as if the cave stretched on for miles with no outlet.

I watched my footing so that I wouldn't trip over rocks jutting up from the cave floor or slip across mud. I quickly started to notice that the tunnel was dipping lower and lower, taking us further down beneath the surface of the earth.

"How far do you think—?"

Ryland was cut off by the roar of rushing water, as if a dam had just broken.

We all exchanged a quick glance before Venn cursed. "Run!" he yelled.

We all broke into a sprint. Water rushed by my boots, passing me. My feet slapped against the ground, spraying up water as I ran. Collectively, we picked up speed, but there was still no end in sight.

"Christ!" Teagan cursed. "How long is this freaking tunnel?"

"I can feel... another enchantment... not far ahead..."

Sondra said through heavy breaths. "Just keep up the pace... and we should—"

Sondra's feet slipped out from under her, and I nearly went down behind her as my boot skidded along the slick cave floor. Venn quickly wrapped his arms under Sondra's and pulled her to her feet, but a second later, the wall of water caught up to us.

The water swept me off my feet like a giant beast swiping at my ankles. Within a split second, I was tumbling through the strong current. I couldn't see anything, even when I tried to open my eyes. My back slammed into the side of the cave before the water caught me again and sucked me downward like a sink drain.

My lungs burned in protest, and my hands instinctively shot out, as if I might be able to find some relief and control my momentum. But relief didn't come. Only pain as the skin on my hands skidded against sharp rocks. On instinct, my lungs opened to fill with air, but they were only assaulted by the sharp pain of water burning up my nostrils. I didn't know where Venn was. I didn't know where anyone was. For the brief time the current took hold of me like Mother Nature's beast, I was completely alone.

My stomach jumped up to my throat as the sensation of falling washed over me. Suddenly, the current was gone. I was suspended in the water, finally gaining control of my movements again. But I had no sense of which way was up or which way was down. Panic shot through my chest, sending my heart pounding so hard that I could hear it pulsing in my ears. I did all I knew I could to save myself. I kicked my feet and swiped my arms through the water, hoping beyond hope that I wasn't pushing myself deeper underwater.

My lungs were on the verge of imploding when my head

broke the surface. I gulped in a greedy breath of air. Relief washed over me so fast that I thought I might cry.

Four headlamps shone back at me, and the tension in my shoulders immediately eased. We were all safe.

Spotting Venn, I swam forward as fast as I could. He'd wrapped me in his arms before I could even fling my hands around his neck. Water brimmed in my eyes, and it wasn't cave water, either.

"Thank God!" Teagan cried in relief as she swam toward Ryland and Sondra.

Ryland hugged her, but his eyes were on his sister. "Are you okay, Fiona?"

Fiona coughed, but she nodded her little fox head.

Venn reached out and wiped a long strand of wet hair from my face. I glanced around while we treaded water. Beyond the headlamps, there was nothing but darkness. Even when I looked upward, all I saw was black. A jet of water spewed out of a tunnel above us. All around us spanned an underground lake inside a massive cavern.

"I see shore," Sondra stated, pointing.

The shore was barely visible in the dim light. The closer we swam, the more I could make it out. There were only a few yards of shoreline before the ground met up with the cave wall, where six separate tunnels split off in different directions.

By the time we reached the thin beach, I was physically exhausted. I fell to my back on the cave floor, not caring that my pack was uncomfortable on my back. I inhaled deep, audible breaths.

"I need a quick break," I said as I pushed myself to a sitting position and pulled my pack onto my lap. I reached inside for a drink of water and a granola bar, hoping it wasn't soaked. I rifled through the contents, past a first-aid kit in a water-tight container and another rope, until I found a granola bar that looked safe to eat.

"We'll take five minutes," Sondra agreed. "But let's hurry, because this cavern is heavily enchanted, and—"

I never got to hear the rest of Sondra's sentence. My entire body gave a jolt of terror. Pain shot through my skull as cold fingers tangled in my hair and dragged me backward into the depths of the deep, dark tunnel behind me.

An earth-shattering scream ripped out of my lungs. "Venn!" The light from my headlamp darted across the rock above me, but I was moving so fast that the cave ceiling was just a blur. My fingers dug into the dirt beneath me, and sharp rocks skidded along my lower back, biting at the skin between my shirt and jeans.

When I found no relief clawing at the ground, my hands shot above my head and clamped around damp, cold flesh. My fingernails sliced into the creature's wrist. It responded in a high-pitched hiss, but it didn't let me go. It continued to drag me by the hair, nearly tugging my ponytail out of my scalp.

"*Ardeat ignis!*" I shouted, but the fire I expected never came.

Shit. How am I supposed to let go of negative energy at a time like this?

I squeezed tighter on the creature's wrist, using all the strength I had, but it still didn't drop me. What the hell was this thing? Its wrists should be broken by now.

"Let go of me, you mother—" I kicked my feet off the

ground and twisted. Hair ripped from my scalp, but I was no longer being dragged. I quickly sprang to my feet. All I saw was a shadow the size of a child as I kicked the creature with all my strength. It went flying across the tunnel.

Then my light caught it. It was less than half my size, with hairless, translucent skin the color of dirty dishwater. It was bipedal, with long nails growing from its human-like fingers. Its eyes were mere pin-pricks, and its ears were just holes in the side of its head. It had a flat nose and a row of sharp, razor-like teeth. My breath wavered at the sight of it.

A deep, guttural bark resounded through the cave. A moment later, the shadow of a large canine crossed my light's path. A low *thud* met my ears as Venn leapt forward in wolf form to fight off the creature made of nightmares.

The creature showed no fear. It leapt forward and sank its nails into Venn's snout. Venn shook his head violently, whipping the creature off of him. It slammed into the cave wall so hard that the rock above us shook. I expected it to fall to the ground unconscious, but it sprang right back up and lunged for Venn again as if it'd felt nothing.

Bile rose to my throat when I saw that the first creature was the least of our problems. At least fifty others crept into the light. Their muscles twitched unnaturally as they moved, making them look like something from a horror movie.

They can go straight to hell.

Venn let out a howl as the creature's sharp teeth tore at the flesh on his front paw. Bones crunched. Venn immediately lunged forward, his jaws snapping until they clamped around the freaky thing's throat. Though it let out a low sigh as it went limp, it didn't bleed.

The being vanished from between Venn's jaws upon its

death. Which could only mean one thing. These creatures were made of magic.

Taking a deep breath in through my nose, I released the air out through my mouth. *This better work.*

"Venn," I whispered, holding out a hand cautiously.

He looked to me, his wolf eyes glowing back at me.

"Step away slowly," I instructed.

Venn followed my gaze and noticed the other cave creatures approaching us for the first time. His body tensed, but he retreated with careful steps. The beings eyed us with interest, inching closer and closer with each passing second.

"When I say so, get ready to run," I warned.

Venn nodded.

I waited until the creatures were only a few yards away. "Now!" I screamed just before shouting the incantation for fire.

Orange flames shot out of my hands like an explosion, assaulting the creatures. Heat touched my face. I just barely saw the beings scurrying away before I turned and ran behind Venn.

The light from three other headlamps bobbed in the distance. Venn shifted as soon as we met up with the others.

Sondra reached me first and placed her hands on my cheeks, looking me over with panic in her eyes. "Are you okay?"

"Yes," I said, glancing behind me to make sure we weren't being followed. "But Venn isn't."

I shrugged my bag off my shoulders as Venn shifted. Teagan was immediately at his side, inspecting his bleeding hand.

"What happened?" Ryland demanded breathlessly.

I pulled the first-aid kit from my backpack and stole

another glance down the tunnel. It was completely deserted, but that didn't keep me from working quickly in case they were on their way.

Venn slumped against the wall and sank down to the ground. He sucked in a sharp breath and closed his eyes, looking weak and worn out. The cut was deep. He was losing a lot of blood.

I gently took Venn's hand and began wrapping gauze tightly around it. "We were attacked by these… things. I don't know what the hell they were."

"They didn't bleed," Venn said in a labored tone. "And one disappeared like a vampire when I killed it."

Sondra knelt beside him and whispered an incantation under her breath. I wasn't sure if it was to help with the pain or restore his energy, but as soon as she finished, he opened his eyes, looking more alert.

"Here," Sondra said, shoving a water bottle toward him. She gently lifted it to his lips, forcing him to drink. "How are you feeling?"

"Better," Venn admitted once she drew the water bottle away from him.

"What about you, Sondra?" I asked with concern. She was starting to look a little pale. "You look like you're exerting too much energy."

She waved a hand like it didn't matter. "I'm fine. I'm a high witch. I can handle a lot of magic."

Except something told me that despite her ability to cast complicated spells, she didn't have the stamina to cast them all at once.

"You said they disappeared?" Sondra asked, redirecting the conversation.

"Yes," Venn confirmed as he stood.

I shoved the first-aid kit back in my pack and rose to my feet beside him.

"I've heard of these things before," Sondra said. "They're the enchantment I felt back by the lake. I'm sure of it."

"What are they?" Teagan asked.

"Mongrels," Sondra answered. "Mongrels come in various forms and can look like almost anything. They're a physical manifestation of a spell that's used to scare people. The spell is usually used to protect something valuable, which definitely fits the bill in this case."

"Why haven't we ever heard of them?" Ryland asked.

"Because the spell is incredibly rare and difficult to cast," Sondra explained. "But they only appear in front of the scared and the weak."

"I was exhausted when we came out of the lake," I said. "Is that why it attacked me?"

Sondra nodded. "Yeah, that makes sense. I know how hard this sounds, you guys, but you can't let your fear get to you in here. The more scared you are, the more chance there is of running into the mongrels again—and who knows what else."

"I thought you said a little fear was a healthy thing," Teagan pointed out.

Sondra hesitated a moment. "I did… But this is not exactly a test of fear. It is a test of faith. We're safe by each other's sides. I promise you that. I'm going to get each and every one of you out of here. You have nothing to be afraid of."

Venn took a breath and nodded. "Agreed. I trust Sondra. I trust all of you. We've got this."

The weight on my chest lifted. "So, now that the mongrels are gone, where do we go? There were six tunnels by the lake. Do you think one leads to the Artifact?"

"Yes," Sondra said. "I don't feel anything down this tunnel

anymore, so let's go back and see if we can feel something down one of the others."

We started down the tunnel back the way we came. After a good five minutes, I was starting to worry.

"This is the way we came, isn't it?" I asked. "I wasn't even dragged for a minute. Was the mongrel *that* fast?"

"No," Sondra replied, glancing around the tunnel. "We should've been back at the lake by now. I didn't see another tunnel. Did anyone else?"

Everyone shook their heads.

"Crap," Sondra muttered.

"What?" Venn demanded. "What's going on?"

Sondra's eyes remained locked ahead. I followed her gaze to see the tunnel widen into a small cavern no bigger than a bedroom. Five other tunnels broke off in all directions like the ones back at the lake. It was clear we were no longer in the right tunnel.

Sondra spun as we entered the cavern, taking it all in. "There's no telling where these tunnels lead. Be prepared to question everything you see down here."

"What are you saying?" Teagan asked.

Sondra let out a heavy breath. "We've just entered an impossible labyrinth."

"What do we do?" Ryland demanded, as if Sondra navigated changing labyrinths daily.

"The important thing is that we stick together," Sondra said. "If we end up down different tunnels, we may never find each other again."

Teagan peered into each tunnel. They were all equally dark and ominous. "What's the trick?"

"Trick?" Sondra asked.

"Yeah, the trick," Teagan replied with a wave of her hand. "How do we make sure the tunnels stop changing and always lead to the same destination? How do we decide which one holds the Artifact?"

"I'm not sure we *can* stop it from changing," Sondra replied. "This is just a wild guess, but I think what we're looking at is Synchrony on steroids."

"Huh?" I asked.

"Synchrony reflects your intentions back on you," Sondra explained. "Positivity breeds positivity. A labyrinth like this will do the same thing, but with different energy signatures."

"So you're saying fear will breed fear?" Venn theorized.

"Exactly," Sondra confirmed. "That's what the mongrels are. They will take any shape to scare you. But I have a feeling that's not the only thing we'll encounter down here."

"Examples?" Ryland pressed.

Sondra shrugged. "It could be anything. If all you're focusing on is how you'll never get out of here, you'll never find an exit. So I suggest you try to let go of worries."

Teagan scoffed. "Easy for you to say. You've had lifetimes of practice."

Sondra frowned. "I never said it was easy. Keep your thoughts positive and we shouldn't have any issues. And if you *do* end up victim of the labyrinth, I suggest you find a way to turn your thoughts around. We'll start down this tunnel."

Sondra began toward the tunnel on the left side of the one we came through. Ryland and Teagan exchanged a glance before following behind her, putting Venn and me in the back.

"Sondra's very optimistic," I said as Venn and I fell into step side by side.

"She tries to be empathetic, but I think she forgets sometimes how hard it can be to control yourself," he replied.

I kept my eyes on Fiona's red fur in front of me. "I know what you mean about losing control. Put a vampire in front of me and a sharp object in my hand and you can bet he's not leaving except in a pile of ashes."

Venn laughed lightly. "You get a pass for vampire slaying. Nobody can resist a good fight." He shot me a teasing smile.

"Well, let's just hope we don't get split up because"—I glanced behind me to see the room we'd left was just barely visible in the distance—"I wouldn't want to be the sucker who has to navigate this labyrinth alone…"

I turned back toward Venn, but my light hit nothing

except the rocky cave wall. As my light swept the tunnel, I found that I was completely alone. When I glanced back to the tunnel room, that was gone, too. It was nothing but a long, dark tunnel with no end in either direction.

I should've been scared shitless at everyone's sudden disappearance, and maybe I would've if Sondra hadn't just explained the nature of the caves. Instead, all I felt was annoyance sink in my gut.

"Well, shit," I muttered. "I'm officially a sucker. I always did hate mazes."

I continued the way I was originally headed, hoping I'd run into something worthwhile eventually. Maybe I'd stumble upon the Artifact. Or at least make it back to the lake or circle around to the tunnel room. Then I could wait until someone showed up again—hopefully.

But the fact was this tunnel led nowhere. It just went on and on without even rising or falling a degree. I was pretty sure I'd walked past the same rock jutting out of the wall fifty times. I'd stopped to rest three times and ate all my granola bars. I must've been walking half the day. My feet were starting to hurt, and I was in serious need of a nap.

I stopped walking and sank down the wall to the cave floor. What happened back there? Was Venn worried about me?

It's just one of the labyrinth's tricks, I told myself. I needed to focus less on how much I'd been walking, how much my feet hurt, and how freaking lonely this vast tunnel was. Like Sondra had instructed, I had to turn my thoughts around.

"Positive thoughts... positive thoughts..." I repeated, closing my eyes. "I *will* find Venn..."

I half expected to hear his voice calling in the distance. I peeked one eye open, but nothing had changed.

I squeezed my eyes shut again. "I will find the end of this tunnel. I will get out of here."

And when I do, the first thing I'm doing is ordering a juicy double bacon cheeseburger, because I'm starving.

This time when my eyes opened, I noticed a glimmer of light at the end of the tunnel. I shot to my feet, squinting to make it out. I turned off my headlamp just to be sure, and sure enough, the light continued to flicker across the cave walls like a flame.

I hurried forward, eager to finally escape this endless tunnel. The light grew brighter and brighter as I approached, until I broke free of the tunnel and stepped into a vast cavern with a tall ceiling. The cavern was the size of a gymnasium, with long wooden tables spanning the length of it. Each table was set with hundreds of flickering candles placed between plate upon plate of chocolate cake. My mouth watered.

"Very funny!" I shouted to no one in particular.

It was official. I was going insane. Could that happen after only a few hours? Or had it been longer? My stomach rumbled like I hadn't eaten for days. The endless chocolate cake stared back at me, tempting me to gobble it up like Thanksgiving dinner.

But I had more sense than to eat random pieces of cake inside an enchanted labyrinth. It'd probably poison me, or turn me into a frog or something. Still, I found myself stepping toward the closest plate. What would it hurt to take just a little bite?

My gaze caught a fork I hadn't noticed before, and I

reached for it. Sure, I could resist one of the most powerful objects in the world, but when it came to chocolate, I was done for.

I'm not going to eat it, I decided. *I'm just going to smell it.*

My fork plunged into the cake, and I tore a moist corner off. Small white pebbles poured out of the cake from where I'd broken it. At least, I thought they were pebbles… until they started squirming.

Maggots!

The labyrinth was sticking up her middle finger at me.

"Nasty!" I stuck mine up right back and skewered the suckers with my fork.

The maggots I stabbed only broke apart and multiplied. Suddenly, maggots exploded out of hundreds of cakes around me. There were so many that they covered the tables and fell to the floor.

Disgusting!

I gagged and whirled around to race back toward the tunnel. It was just behind me when I entered the room, but now it was a good fifty yards away. I pushed forward, squashing maggots with my feet as I went.

Ew, ew, ew!

I trudged through the pool of maggots that were up to my knees now. Why did it have to be *maggots?* They were only second on my hit list after vampires. They were hands down one of the most disgusting creatures on the planet.

Suddenly, they started jumping, as if they were some sort of mutant maggots. I could already feel them squirming against my legs. No way in hell was I taking one up the nose.

The tunnel seemed farther away than ever, and my heart began to pound like I was never going to make it. These suckers were going to crawl inside my throat, choke me, then eat me before my body had a chance to cool.

Not on my watch.

Ignoring my instinct not to touch them, I pressed my hands to the nearest maggot-infested table. Their little bodies squished under my weight while others wiggled their way onto my skin. I pulled myself onto the table, freeing my legs from the swarm of maggots at my feet and shaking off the others. I quickly jumped up and raced down the table, kicking plates as I went.

The only thing that would make this worse is a...

I didn't get a chance to finish my thought before the cavern began rumbling. The table shook beneath my feet, and a pile of rocks crumbled down a tall slope in the wall to my right. Bile rose in my throat. I told myself to not look back, but I couldn't help it. I had to see for myself.

I dared a glance behind my shoulder as I ran. What I saw stole my attention, which sent me tripping over a plate and into the pile of maggots. I caught my fall, squishing guts out of their little white bodies and between my fingers.

But maggot guts were the least of my worries. Behind me, the holy mother of all larvae rose up. It was as big as a semi-truck. Its tall brown head nearly touched the ceiling of the cave. Six legs protruded from its fat, slimy white body and wiggled in the air. In the candlelight, it looked freaky and disgusting as shadows rippled across its body. It let out a deep roar akin to Ryland's. Which was totally weird, because I didn't think maggots made a sound. But maggots weren't exactly the size of semi-trucks, either. It must've been a product of the labyrinth's mind games meant to scare me. Which, by the way, was kind of working.

This is apparently what I get for being a Negative Nancy.

Control your damn thoughts, girl! Except I couldn't just think away the giant vermin. God, this enchanted cave was confusing as hell.

I grabbed the first thing my hands could find, which happened to be a plate. I sprang to my feet and chucked it at the giant maggot's head. I didn't stick around to see where it hit. I whirled toward the tunnel I came through and took off sprinting—only, the tunnel wasn't there anymore. Worry ripped through me involuntarily.

You can't worry, Rachel! It'll only make it worse. Think positive thoughts. Rainbows. Butterflies. Sunshine.

Even my own mini pep talk was *so* not helping me right now.

I glanced behind me just in time to see the giant maggot lunging toward me, as if it was going to grab me between its pinchers and gobble me up for its next meal.

Oh, no you don't.

I quickly dodged out of the way, leaping over the pile of baby maggots on the ground and to the next table. Big ol' Mother Maggot crashed into the table I'd just been running down. It collapsed beneath her weight. I promptly leapt to the next table, and then the one after that, to put as much distance between myself and Mother Maggot as possible. My eyes darted around the cave, desperately searching for an exit.

Mother Maggot isn't getting her next meal. I'll fight to the death if I have to.

My eyes fell upon a tunnel on the other side of the room. Problem was, Mother Maggot was right between me and my chance of escape. She rose up again, showing off her size and staring down at me with eyes I was sure were there—but couldn't see. They must've been just pin pricks. Her jaws snapped at me. Taking a deep breath, I swooped down and grabbed a fork in each hand. She wasn't a vampire, and these forks weren't exactly knives, but this bitch was begging for a fight. And she was going down.

"Can't we compromise?" I said aloud, as if Mother Maggot could actually understand me. "You let me go free and I don't kill you?"

She didn't even hesitate. She threw herself forward again. I ducked and rolled out of the way, crushing hundreds of baby maggots. I felt the wind rush past her and the table buckle under her weight. She groaned. WTF? Maggots don't groan. What kind of freaky cave was this?

My gaze darted to where the tunnel had just been, but instead of finding it where I expected, it had moved. Even though Mother Maggot and I had changed directions, my escape tunnel was still on the opposite side of her.

Which only meant one thing. The labyrinth wanted a show.

I couldn't help but let out a low laugh. It was probably mostly because I was tired and hungry and a bit on the loopy side, but it felt damn good to laugh. "You're on."

Mother Maggot was already rising up again. I jumped forward and leapt onto her back. She was slippery, but her skin had ridges that I could hold on to. Pulling back my arm, I jabbed my fork into her skin. It did nothing but bounce off of her.

Okay...

Mother Maggot began thrashing her body from side to side, trying to throw me off of her. I held on tighter. In a last-ditch effort, she threw herself to the ground. The impact shook her whole body, and I could no longer hold on. I fell into a pile of baby maggots. Before I could jump back to my feet, Mother Maggot's body came into view. She was rolling over, and she was going to squash me!

I ignored the baby maggots and scrambled to my feet, digging them into the ground and diving out of the way. I just barely missed being pinned beneath her body. Glancing around for a weapon, I grabbed the closest thing my fingers could find—one of the flaming candles. Just as I turned around to use it on her, Mother Maggot's legs clamped around me.

I screamed in surprise as she lifted me into the air, but she squeezed me so tightly that my scream was cut off within a second. I lifted the candle to burn the closest area of flesh I could find, which happened to be one of her legs.

Mother Maggot cried out in pain, sounding a lot like a whale in labor—not that I was exactly familiar with that sound. She loosened the one leg and snapped her jaws at me again. My arm slipped free, and I jabbed the candle straight into her face between where I guessed her eyes would be.

She stumbled backward, loosening her grip on me just enough that I could get my hands on one of her legs and twist as hard as I could. The cry only grew louder, and her hold on me weakened, but she didn't let me go. Mother Maggot stumbled and twisted, until we both went crashing into the cave wall. She caught herself with her top legs, but it wasn't enough to keep the air from knocking out of my lungs.

As I sucked in deep breaths, my eyes fell upon the huge rock pile beside us. Just before she could right herself, I reached out and grabbed the closest rock I could find. To my surprise, it was a sharp, pointed rock. Just what I needed.

I smiled cunningly. Mother Maggot lowered her jaw, aiming her open mouth at my head. Now that I had my lucky rock, I wasn't even worried. I drew my arm back and plunged that sucker straight into her chest.

A high-pitched shriek echoed off the cave walls. She finally let me go, but I held on to that rock with dear life as I dropped to the ground. It sliced through her all the way down. Guts spilled onto the cave floor, covering me in a fresh layer of goop.

But I didn't care. Mother Maggot's body slumped against the rock pile. I was free. I smiled triumphantly, but I didn't stick around to revel in the victory. I dropped my rock and whirled around, sprinting straight for the tunnel before it could move again. I didn't slow down until I knew the room of rotten nightmares was far behind me.

When the light from the room faded and the tunnel was covered in pitch blackness again, I finally slowed. I took a knee to catch my breath and turned my headlamp back on. Now that that nightmare was over, I needed to figure something out—and fast. Frankly, I was already sick of this labyrinth and its little mind games. If I didn't learn how to play this game to my favor, I'd be trapped here forever.

The earth rumbled beneath me, and my eyes instantly darted around the tunnel. My heart hammered violently as I shot to my feet. If I thought Mother Maggot was bad, it was nothing compared to this. The cave walls were inching closer and closer together, the space around me shrinking right before my eyes like some sort of Scooby-Doo boobytrap shit.

My time to play my cards had run out. If I didn't figure out my move in the next twenty seconds, the labyrinth was going to crush me.

19

Sondra's words echoed in my head. *If you do end up victim of the labyrinth, I suggest you find a way to turn your thoughts around.*

How the heck was I supposed to turn my thoughts around? Panic settled in as my headlamp hit a rocky ceiling that was closing in on me inch by inch each passing second.

Run, instinct told me, but there was nowhere to go. The whole tunnel was shrinking, with no way out.

"No, no, no, no," I cried as I reached my hands to either side of the tunnel. Both of my hands touched rock, and I locked my elbows as if I could hold the rock back. Even with my super shifter strength, I couldn't hold back the freaking earth.

So instead, I closed my eyes, plugged my ears with my fingers, and squatted down, curling into a ball. All I needed was to take my mind off of the shrinking tunnel. The labyrinth reflected my thoughts and worries back on me, right? I just had to stop worrying.

Shit! This is hard.

My mind flickered through thought after thought as I forced myself to ignore the impending danger surrounding me. *Venn, Jenna, Fiona, ice cream, spell books, vampires, venom...*

Why the heck were these the first things to flicker through my mind? This wasn't working!

It was like trying to wish away the monster under my bed as a kid...

And that's when it struck me. That was all this labyrinth was. A maze of monsters of my own making. And there was only one way to get rid of the monsters.

I began singing. Though it was horribly off key, my mind slipped back to a memory I hadn't recalled in years. My mother sat on the side of my bed, running her fingers through my hair while I held the edge of the blanket up past my nose. Her beautiful voice filled my bedroom.

The full moon is shining
The stars glitter above
The wind whispers softly
Goodnight, my love

I repeated the lullaby again, rocking back and forth ever so slightly as the melody filled my heart and made me think of home. All my fears flashed across my eyelids in a split second: getting crushed to death here in this cave, standing in front of Jenna's gravestone if I ever made it out of here, hearing Venn tell me the family didn't want me around anymore, getting bit by a vampire and waking up with silver eyes and a thirst for blood...

But I pushed all of those fears away as the memory of my mother's eyes overshadowed them. I thought of my dad's tight hugs and the way he would tickle my feet to cheer me up, even when I was a teen and refused to smile for him. One time, Jenna joined in and they tickled me so hard that I kicked her in the face and she had to go to the emergency room. It turned out her nose wasn't broken, so Dad took us both out for ice cream afterward to celebrate her "miraculous recovery."

A tear fell down my cheek as I continued singing the lullaby. Not because I was scared anymore, but because I missed those times with my family. I missed them so badly it hurt. The best I could do now was be thankful for what little time I had with them and never let their memory die.

I am strong. I am resilient. I will make it out of here.

As the last line of the lullaby passed my lips another time, I suddenly realized that the walls of the cave should've crushed me by now. Slowly, I lifted my head and peeled my eyes open. A sigh of relief whooshed out of my lungs when I saw that the tunnel had widened back to its original size. I let out a nervous half-cry, half-laugh.

"Thank you!" I shouted to the labyrinth. I rushed over to the wall of the cave and kissed it. "Thank you for not crushing me!"

I started down the tunnel, feeling hopeful about what was at the end of it. Sondra had said I needed to find something that would work for me to calm me down to perform magic. I was pretty sure the lullaby from my childhood was it. Which was weird because I couldn't sing worth a damn, but hey, if it kept me from getting crushed in a booby-trapped tunnel, I was all for it.

"Okay, labyrinth," I said aloud. My voice echoed down the tunnel. "I've almost drowned, fought off your mongrels, got lost for hours, faced one of my worst nightmares, and just survived almost being crushed to death. I don't give up that easily. Bring on your next move! I'll take on whatever you've got until I find that artifact."

As if in answer, my headlamp caught a dark, open cavern ahead. I couldn't see what lay beyond the opening, but I rushed forward to find out. The closer I came to it, the more I could feel the energy from a strong enchantment buzzing through the air. Whatever was in there was powerful. I slowed when I reached the end of the tunnel.

As soon as I stepped into the room, a thousand candles lining the rocky walls lit up, as if I'd set off a motion sensor. I drew in a breath as my eyes spanned the cave. It wasn't huge, perhaps the size of a large bedroom, but the ceiling stretched up at least fifty feet above my head. The only way out was through the tunnel behind me. Layers upon layers of rock jutted out from the walls, creating flat surfaces for the candles to sit.

In the middle of it all stood a naturally formed rock pedestal. On top of that was the object radiating the magic I felt in the tunnel.

Sapiens noctua. The Wise Owl.

It wasn't like the marble carving in the Genevieve's test. It was an honest-to-God real owl skull. I stepped closer to it and reached out my hand cautiously, as if I thought it might burn me. As soon as my fingers clamped around the skull, a jolt of magic shot through me like a lightning bolt.

I crumbled to my knees, and though I was pretty sure I let out a cry, I couldn't process it. Magic pulsed through me at all angles like I was standing between two massive stereo speakers at high volume. It didn't hurt, really, but it was uncomfortable and overwhelming. The power I felt rushing through the Artifact was ten times that of what I felt in Genevieve's test.

Somewhere through my clouded mind, my thoughts broke through. *Do something, Rachel.*

What did I mean? What was I supposed to do?

Focus.

"*The full moon is shining...*" I started, but the words fell from my mind as the magic intensified, pulsing stronger through my body.

Shit. Where was I? What's going on?

I barely remembered I was in the cave at all. It felt like I was in a billion different places at once—that I was a billion different people with a billion different thoughts racing through my head. I couldn't differentiate my own thoughts from all the other voices whispering in my mind. A single thought stuck out in the sea of noise.

Control it!

This power was too much. If I didn't push back, it was going to rip me apart.

Except... how did I control it? I was only a low witch. I didn't have this kind of power.

You do. Everyone keeps telling you that you're more powerful than you think. It's time to start believing it.

"Gah!" I screamed as the magic pushed in on me, as if trying to crush me.

So much power. You could do anything. Be anything.

Yeah, another voice countered. *You could be dead.*

That thought immediately made me more alert, pushing all the other voices to the back of my mind. I was looking into the heart of Synchrony. Surely with the power to flip the switch on anyone's magic, I could find a way to dull my own, to control it.

But before I do...

I knew it was stupid of me to dive deeper, but the temptation was too great. Even if it killed me, I *had* to know.

I sifted through the voices, through the energy signatures I now had access to. I flipped through them faster than a computer could process data, searching for the one that was most familiar to me after my own.

Her energy felt like velvet and smelled of sweet apples. There was a roughness around the edges that I was unfamiliar with, but there was no doubt it was her. A sensation that felt a lot like my own shifter magic tingled through me, and an image of Jenna's face flickered across my closed lids.

She's alive.

That was all I needed from the Artifact. I had no desire to control the rest of its power, and so I pushed it away. It was like trying to push a thousand-ton boulder off a cliff, but slowly and surely, the power eased, and the voices softened. They were still there, but they were like whispers behind the brick wall I'd built in my mind.

I forced my eyes open. The cave floor swam in front of me, but my knees felt steady on the ground.

And then the sound of clapping met my ears. My heart leapt into my throat. I whirled around, my hands already curled into fists in front of me. The last person I expected to see stepped out from the shadows of the tunnel and into the candlelight.

Matias Vayne.

20

Matias looked exactly like he had the first time I saw him, all suited up with perfect hair and that damn attractive jawline. *It's just another trick*, I told myself.

"Well done, Rachel," he said, stepping further into the room.

"Nice one," I said, rolling my eyes. "But I'm not scared of this dude." I eyed him up and down. Even if he were really here, I figured I'd stand a chance against him.

Matias's eyebrows shot up. "You think I'm a hallucination? A part of the enchantment put on these caves?"

He took another step forward. I planted my feet firmly in place, leveling him with a challenging gaze.

"You are, aren't you?" I accused.

Matias gestured to himself. "I'm as real as they get, sweetheart. You know, the funny thing about these caves is that you can never quite tell which parts are real and which ones are only in your head. The mongrels, for example… those bastards will kill you. The rest… well, that's just for fun."

"And which are you?" I asked coolly. "Are you just for fun, or are you the killing type?"

Matias took another step forward but turned to a candle beside him. He ran his fingers across the top of the flame, as if he needed something to do with his hands. He laughed lightly. "We can have fun if you're in to that, but I assure you this is not the killing kind of visit."

He was *so* wrong. He was a vampire. Vampire visits were always the killing kind. Not to mention that he wanted the Artifact, which I was bound and determined to destroy, *and* he was standing between me and my only chance of escape. I only had one choice.

"Yeah, well," I countered, "it's the killing kind of visit for me."

I lunged forward, intending to clip him in the jaw, but he reacted quickly and dodged out of the way. The bastard was smart and kept himself between me and the tunnel, ensuring I couldn't just turn around and run. So I aimed a foot at him instead. He let out a grunt as my heel connected with his abdomen. In the blink of an eye, his hands shot out and clamped around my ankle before I could get it out of his reach. He squeezed tightly and twisted. I let the momentum take me, grabbing on to one of the long candles on the ledge behind me as I spun. My other foot connected with his cheek as I went crashing to the ground. He smirked in satisfaction when he saw me lying there, but it only lasted a split-second before I shoved the burning candle up into his face.

He reeled backward, giving me just enough time to jump to my feet. Clutching the Artifact in one hand, I rushed toward the tunnel. He had a hold of my wrist in under a second, and he whirled me around until he was between me and the tunnel again. I swung my knee up *hard*, sinking my knee into his royal jewels.

Damn, that was satisfying.

The vamp was too focused on baring his fangs at me to even flinch.

Seeing as I didn't have a weapon handy, I did the only other thing I could think of. I shifted, abandoning my backpack, and scooped up the owl skull with my talons. I flew high above his head and swooped down toward the tunnel. He spun away from me and raced toward the rock ledges, using them to gain height. Before I made it to tunnel, he was soaring through the air, reaching for me.

His hands caught my leg and tugged at my lower feathers as he dragged me out of the air and whipped me across the room. My body slammed into the rock walls, and The Wise Owl fell from my talons.

I shifted back to human form and grabbed the skull before he could get to it. I breathed heavily as I took a defensive stance. I kept my eyes on him, but I focused on my peripheral vision, hoping to spot a loose rock or something to use against him.

And then I realized… I was holding one of the most powerful objects in existence in my hand. I could just flip the switch on his vampire magic that was keeping him alive and kill him. Right? Was that how it worked? No harm in trying it.

"I just want to talk," he said, holding out a hand as if trying to reason with a wild dog.

"About what?" I demanded. "How can I even be sure you're real?"

Matias relaxed, standing straighter. "Do you really think I'd be anywhere else, that I wouldn't have found you?"

I hesitated. "I don't know how you did. The locket only works when—"

"Pfft," Matias scoffed. "I wasn't talking about the locket. I had eyes on you the whole time. As soon as I received the locket and saw that you were going after the Artifact, I sent my men after you. But my men you attacked on the street weren't the only ones watching."

I searched for his energy signature while he spoke, but his words halted me in my tracks. Now he had me intrigued.

"You let Sondra overhear you, knowing she'd find it?" I guessed.

Matias nodded. "I had a hunch. She always was easy to manipulate. I needed a witch who could find these caves and open the passageway. Luckily for me, you did all the work; I just had to follow and make sure you didn't turn back."

I drew in a sharp breath, though I tried not to let it show. "You're the reason the entrance caved in, aren't you?"

Matias smirked. "Guilty. I couldn't have you giving up when you were so close."

"Why go after the locket in the first place if all you ever wanted was this?" I sneered.

Matias leaned an elbow against one of the rock ledges, looking amused. "I never said it didn't come in handy. It is quite a useful object if you know how to use it. Imagine my surprise when you, Rachel Collins, showed up to deliver it."

Nausea hit my gut. "How do you know my name?"

Matias smirked. "I have an unlimited amount of resources. What would you rather I call you? Ravenite, perhaps?"

The blood drained from my face.

He must've noticed my expression, because he straightened and shrugged. "Like I said, unlimited resources, my dear. You have quite the reputation, don't you?"

My jaw tensed, and I spoke in warning. "Yes. I'm very good at killing vampires."

"Of course," he said with a nod. "You've spent many lifetimes cleaning up the mess you made."

"Excuse me?" I snapped.

My magic honed in on his energy signature. It felt rough like rock and smelled of burning oil. I was ready to cut off his magic at any point. But I couldn't bring myself to do it until I heard what he had to say. How did he know so much about me?

"Oh, you don't know?" His eyebrows shot up, and he clicked his tongue. "Rachel, Rachel, Rachel… I must say, I'm a little disappointed in you. I mean, if someone like *me* can remember my past lives before Valkas returned, I would've expected much more from you. Though you were… what? Ten or so when it happened."

"What are you talking about?" I demanded. "You couldn't have remembered anything before Valkas escaped. You didn't have the magic to remember."

Matias let out a fake sigh, as if amused. "Oh, sweetheart. You're like a child all over again. How about a history lesson?"

He didn't give me a chance to answer before continuing. "Magic never completely disappeared with Valkas. It only weakened. I mean, we still had psychics, healers, and things like that. We saw magic in a different way. Some people called it luck. Others called it miracles. I called it hard work and perseverance. How else would I have built the empire I have from the ground up?"

He began pacing in front of the tunnel entrance. "I was a strong witch in my past lives. I didn't know it in this life, but I was able to use my natural connection to Synchrony to find success. With each success, I could feel there was something bigger than me, something handing me everything I asked for. I found a diary from my past life that explained everything, about Synchrony, about Valkas—all of it."

My eyebrows shot up. "And you just stumbled upon it?"

He shrugged. "I was drawn to it. Ever have *déjà vu*, Rachel? Ever felt like a place was familiar when you'd never been there before, or recognized someone you'd never met?" He didn't let me answer, but I knew exactly what he meant. "I followed Synchrony like a religion, and the more I came to understand about it, the more I remembered. I was there when we trapped Valkas, and so I could break the spell. I knew how to free him."

I gasped. "It was *you* eight years ago! You're the reason he came back!" My hands curled tighter around the Artifact. As soon as he was done talking, he was dead.

Matias smiled. "Yes."

"Why would you do that!?" I shouted. "Do you know how many people he's killed?"

Matias dropped his gaze. "Yes, and for that I am truly sorry."

I scoffed. "You're a vampire. You have no empathy or remorse."

"I did," Matias shot back at me. "I've done more for this world in my life than you could ever imagine. Do you have any idea how much money I've given to fight poverty? The homes and counseling I've sponsored to save women from domestic violence? The foundations I've set up to fight child-hood hunger? Vampires are the least of your problems. People were destroying each other long before Valkas came along."

"What does any of this have to do with freeing Valkas?" I questioned.

Matias's voice returned to a normal level. "It was never

my intention to let him live. I only freed him to free magic. With it, I knew I could heal the world. But I made a mistake. You see, I thought that breaking a spell only took a piece of what was used to create it. And so, I tracked down the dagger used in the spell to spill Valkas's blood. I tried to kill him as soon as I freed him, but he only pulled the blade from his chest as if nothing had happened. That's when I realized that to break the spell, you didn't *only* need an object used to create it. You also needed the witch who cast it."

"So you freed Valkas, tried to kill him, but he changed you instead," I guessed.

"Yes," Matias said. "Luckily for me, his bloodlust got the best of him, and he wasn't thinking straight. I changed rather than died. I think Synchrony wanted it that way."

"Why? What's your plan now? Take the Artifact and control the world?"

"I wouldn't say control. I will… *improve*."

The way he said it sure didn't sound like it.

"How?" I asked.

"I don't need to go into the specifics," he said with a wave of his hand. "I will create a world with structure… with rules that will be followed without question. The world will finally be at peace."

"By taking away other people's free will." It wasn't a question.

"People don't know how to handle free will!" he shouted. "Look what they've done with it! They rape, they murder, they steal. I will use the Artifact to purify the world. Nobody else is willing to step up and do what has to be done."

Matias had a point, but he was talking about playing God, about using the Artifact as a judgement tool. With control over magic, he could choose who lived and who died. He could control everything...

It wouldn't fix the world. Far from it. It would only give the illusion until someone broke through his chains and decided to fight back. And that sorry sucker was probably going to be me.

That was why this Artifact needed to be destroyed. He wasn't getting anywhere near it.

I'd heard enough. If he wanted to get rid of the tainted hearts plaguing the world, his could be the first to go. I tapped into Synchrony through the Artifact, and I willed the magic keeping him alive to leave his body.

It pulled against me, protesting against my power. I tried again, but it was like running into a wall. And that was when I realized that vampire magic was different. This magic fed into him, whereas witches and shifters pulled from Synchrony at will. I couldn't use The Wise Owl to kill him.

"What's your plan with the vampires?" I asked, acting as if nothing was happening inside of me. "You'll never get rid of evil as long as they're around."

"You act like evil is a vampire trait, Rachel. It's not. It is and always has been a human trait. It only became a mark of vampirism when Valkas's own evil heart tainted the spell that created him. Anyway, that's where you come in."

"What do you mean?" I kept my voice calm, but damn it all if I wasn't burning for him to spill every last detail he knew.

"I told you only the witch who created the vampire curse can break it. It wasn't just luck that you stumbled into my office, Rachel."

I don't stumble.

"You still don't get it, do you?" he asked, eyeing my expression. "What do you know of your past lives?"

I hesitated. "Not much," I answered, feeling uncomfortable, like he was fishing for information.

"Oh, dear. It must be sad that I remember more about your past lives than you do. I recognized you the second I saw you, though it didn't all click until later." It sounded like he was telling the truth.

"I know about my last life," I said, refusing to give him so much satisfaction. "I know I was one of the witches who trapped Valkas with you."

"Of course," Matias said, "but you were so much more than that. Like I said, you've been trying to clean up your mess ever since. First, as Abigail. You created the shifters to fight the vampires. Then as Lily Gregor. It was Lily's idea—*your* idea—to gather us all together to trap Valkas. And now in this life, you fight and kill vampires, because you can't handle the evil you created."

"The evil I created? You're implying that I'm—"

"Elizabeth Martin," Matias cut in. "Precisely. You, Rachel, are the witch who created Valkas."

21

My knees went weak, and my mouth felt like sandpaper. *No way* was I responsible for all of this. He was lying to me. That… or none of this was real. It was the labyrinth toying with me again. Yet, a part of me couldn't help but believe him… like I'd already known it was true.

Matias reached into his jacket. Though I went rigid, I was curious as to what he'd pull out. Damn this intriguing, mysterious man.

"I need your help to make the world a better place," Matias said. Which sounded nice, until you considered his plan for power. He produced a small white towel and began unfolding it. "Will you, Rachel, do the honors of killing Valkas and finally ridding the world of this curse?"

It sounded like he was proposing to me or something. *Sorry, buddy. I'm already taken.*

Matias finished unfolding the towel. Inside lay a silver dagger. I recognized it from the dream I'd had at Amalia's. Which meant he was telling the truth. I'd already started remembering my life as Elizabeth. I'd dreamt of the night I'd used the exact same dagger to spill Valkas's blood and perform the spell that would change our world forever.

"I want you to have this, Rachel," he said. "It's the only way to kill him."

I didn't move. There was too much that didn't add up. Clearly, Matias wanted Valkas dead. Maybe it was out of revenge for changing him, or maybe he just wanted to rid the world of such evil. But it didn't make any sense.

"You talk a good talk," I said, "but you can't convince me that easily. What happens to you when I kill Valkas?"

Matias only shrugged. "I suppose it breaks the spell. Once that magic is no longer keeping me alive, I would die—just as would all the other vampires."

It made the idea of killing Valkas just that much more appealing. Except…

"You're asking me to sign your death certificate," I pointed out. "Why would you want that? What about your plan to cure the world?"

"Vampirism may seem like a blessing. I could do so much with my immortality. But there are far more terrible things about it. The constant bloodlust. The emotional disconnect. Oh, don't look so surprised. I'm very aware that I don't feel empathy these days. And that's a problem. There are human emotions I long to feel again… but just can't no matter how hard I try. Vampirism is truly a curse. Once I'm free of the curse, my successor will take my place and carry out my plan."

He sounded so noble, but I wasn't buying it. Maybe at one time he believed he could make the world a better place, but vampires just didn't talk like that… they didn't think like that. They didn't have the empathy he spoke of. I'd run across enough vampires to know there weren't exceptions to the rule. Which meant that whatever Matias's true motivations were went far beyond what he was telling me. He only talked about emotions to manipulate me.

"Come on, Rachel," he encouraged. "Don't you want to avenge your sister?"

My heart stopped at the mention of Jenna. How the hell did he—? *Unlimited resources.* This guy probably hacked into my email accounts and everything.

"Yes," I said slowly… but I couldn't let him go through with his plan. For a better world or not, no one deserved complete power.

First things first, I was getting that dagger. If what he said about it was true—and my gut was saying it was—then I'd need it to get rid of Valkas once and for all.

"I accept your job offer," I said, standing straighter and speaking more confidently.

"Excellent," he replied with a smile.

I stepped forward and held my hand out.

Matias pulled it away. "Give me the Artifact first."

I hesitated. I had no intention of handing it over, but I also needed a weapon if I was going to make it out of here with the Artifact in hand. My options quickly rushed through my head as I contemplated my next move. Chances were Matias had the locket tucked under his shirt and would be able to predict every move I made before I made it. So how the hell was I going to trick him into letting me get away with the owl skull and the dagger? By now he surely knew I wasn't going to let him have it. And if I handed it over and decided to stab him afterward, he'd know that was coming, too.

And so I had to make a choice—one of the hardest decisions I'd ever been asked to make. Would I kill Valkas, effectively destroying the rest of the vampires, and allow another power to rise up—perhaps worse than the last? Or would I let the world continue to spiral down the shithole it was already sinking into? It was a choice between two evils, one I didn't think I was fully prepared to make.

But the answer was obvious to me. I already knew what option I'd choose before I realized I'd decided. This was *Valkas* we were talking about, the man who orchestrated murderers of thousands of people, who wreaked havoc across the country for years, and whose men stole my sister and probably served her for breakfast, lunch, and dinner daily. They were the same men who murdered my parents. He deserved a fate far worse than death. I would trade anything for the chance to drive a dagger through his heart.

My hand stretched out, as if on its own, to offer the Artifact to Matias. In return, he handed me the towel-wrapped dagger.

As soon as the Owl left my hands and the pulse of magic disappeared with it, I realized what a horrible mistake I'd made. What if the world he created was worse than the one we were living in? I had no idea what someone could do if they knew how to leverage The Wise Owl's power.

He smiled. "Excellent. Now—"

I dropped to the ground and swung my leg out at his ankles, catching him completely off guard. His legs whipped out from under him, and he went crashing to the ground. His head caught on one of the rock ledges. I was on top of him in less than a second, my dagger raised and aimed for his heart.

His hand shot out and grabbed my wrist. Holy crap! This guy was stronger than he looked.

"I told you I run fair deals," Matias said as he fought against my arm that pressed toward his chest. "You would make a terrible businesswoman, Rachel."

He threw his hips upward and spun me around until I was

flat on my back. Before I knew it, he was on his feet. His foot pressed down on my chest so hard that I couldn't breathe. I gasped for breath and tightened my hold on the blade.

He leaned down, looming over me as shadows flickered across his face. "I'm not going to kill you, Rachel, so let's stop with the theatrics. We made a fair trade. I'm going to walk out of here with the Artifact, and you're going to go in the opposite direction with the blade. We both get what we want. Understand?"

No way, dickhole!

He wasn't leaving with that artifact as long as I had something to say about it. Unlike him, I never claimed to run clean business deals. I did what was best, and right now, the chance to stop both Valkas *and* Matias looked pretty damn appealing.

In one swift motion, I kicked my foot upward and sliced my blade across his ankle at the same time. My toes connected with the owl skull, sending it flying across the cave. It landed several feet away with a clatter. All within the same second, the weight on my chest lifted.

I inhaled a deep breath as I sprang to my feet then dove for the Artifact. But before I could reach it, Matias's fingers came out of nowhere and snatched it right out from under me.

He took off running down the tunnel. Thinking fast, I grabbed my headlamp that had slid off when I shifted and sprinted behind him. My light bounced off his back as I chased him down the tunnel. The ankle wound had slowed him down, but not enough.

Next time, slice deeper.

Ahead of us, the tunnel split in two directions. Matias took the left path just as a scream of terror ripped through the tunnel on the right.

"Venn!" the female voice shouted.

Sondra.

The family was in trouble.

I skidded to a halt in front of the passageways, hesitating.
Did I go after Matias, or did I help my family?

The choice was impossible to make.

22

My hand squeezed tighter around the blade as I glanced from one tunnel to the other.

"Get off of him, you mother—" The sound of Ryland's roar cut Teagan off.

I didn't have time to stand around contemplating my options. In a split-second decision, I rushed forward and sprinted down the tunnel to my right.

When I broke out of the tunnel, I found myself back on the shore of the underground lake. A shining white orb—some sort of enchantment—hovered high above the lake close to the ceiling, so I could see the chaos in full force. Everything moved so fast that I could barely process it.

Six of Matias's men fought the family, and at least fifty mongrels were clawing at whomever they could get their hands on. Shifters, witches, vampires… it didn't matter to them. They were on no one's side.

I recognized the witch who'd hit Venn with the curse fighting a dozen mongrels alongside the tiger shifter who'd been with him before. Four other vampires were present, two of them taking on Venn in his wolf form. Ryland's jaw snapped at mongrels that were trying to bite him. Teagan sat on his back with Fiona still strapped securely in her pack. She aimed a knife at one of the closest vampires. It landed in his eye socket, sinking through the flesh and into his brain. He disappeared in a pile of ash. His clothes and the knife fell to the floor where he'd vanished.

Five mongrels jumped Sondra at once, dragging her to the ground. She threw her elbow into one of their faces and kicked a knee up into one of their groins.

I rushed toward Sondra since she looked like she needed the most help, but a half dozen mongrels scurried in front of my path. The first one bared its teeth at me and jumped forward, but I kicked that sucker straight out of the air like a soccer ball. He squeaked and went flying. The next one lunged forward with his teeth aimed at my ankles. The freaky little monster wasn't getting anywhere near me. I ducked and sliced my dagger across his throat. He disappeared like the imprint of a ghost washed away with the wind.

Another mongrel jumped on my back, his sharp claws digging into my shoulders. I reached behind myself and grabbed a fistful of the skin on the back of his neck. His claws sliced through my skin as I ripped him off of me, but I barely felt it. Rage and adrenaline shot through me like a flood in an open waterway. A battle cry ripped from my lungs as my dagger sank into the chest of the next mongrel, then sliced the stomach of the one beside him.

Finally clearing a path from me to Sondra, I sprinted for her. She'd managed to take care of most of them, but there was one left and on the verge of biting her face off. I didn't slow as I ran forward and swung my foot out. My foot connected with his gut as I punted him. His hands flew off of

Sondra's shirt, and he went soaring fifteen feet into the air. I quickly offered Sondra my hand and helped her to her feet.

"Thank you," she breathed just before we both spotted another group of mongrels emerging from one of the tunnels and heading straight in our direction. "Go help Venn!" she instructed. "I've got this."

I didn't question her. I whirled around and sprinted toward Venn. Behind me, flashes of white light went off and electricity sizzled through the air as Sondra attacked the mongrels with her lightning power.

A vampire with dark hair held Venn down by his tail, while another with a ratface swung his knee up into Venn's jaw. Ratface's hands tangled in Venn's fur and forced his head back, his fangs heading for Venn's neck. Venn swung his good paw out, slicing his claws against the side of the vamp's face. Ratface pulled back just in time for his eyes to connect with mine as my dagger sank into his friend's back.

"Leave my boyfriend alone!" I snapped as Dark-Haired Vamp disintegrated into a pile of ash.

Ratface smirked. "Gladly. If it means I get you, Ravenite. I bet you taste wonderful."

He was in front of me in a flash. He threw his arm out, and his palm slammed into my chest. My body flew backward and crashed into the cave floor with a hard *thud*.

"Too bad you'll never find out," I said through labored breaths as I swung my leg around, aiming for the back of his knee.

Ratface caught my leg before I could knock him off his feet. I shoved my dagger up into his shin. At the same time, Venn's sharp wolf teeth sank into the vamp's wrist. Ratface let out a scream and dropped my leg. I ripped my dagger from his flesh and sprang to my feet. Venn clamped his jaw tightly around Ratface's arm and swung his head down, pulling Ratface to the ground. A moment of surprise caught his face a split second before my dagger entered his chest.

Venn dipped his head and brushed his fur against my hip, but we didn't have time to enjoy each other's company just yet. Witch Guy and Tiger Shifter had fought off their mongrels and were headed our way. The last vampire had abandoned his fight with Ryland and Teagan to join them. Mongrels flooded out of the caves behind us, most of them headed for the closest target—Ryland, Teagan, and Fiona.

There were too many mongrels to take on at once, not to mention the strongest of Matias's men remaining.

My eyes darted around the cavern, first to Sondra, who was still using lightning to fight off the mongrels. She looked pale and weak, and her lightning was barely visible now as it cracked through the air. She was quickly running out of energy.

On the other side of me, my eyes fell upon the dark lake. It gave me an idea, which was a heck of a long shot but also our only option.

Finally, my gaze fell upon Matias's men stalking confidently our way. Witch Guy's lips moved, though I didn't hear what he'd said. Suddenly, a glowing green ball of energy erupted from his palm, aimed straight for Venn. Venn ducked out of the way, and the spell exploded against the ground behind him. Witch Guy's eyes flickered toward me, but he quickly looked back to Venn, anger etched in his eyes. The vamp and tiger beside him also had their eyes trained on Venn, like they barely noticed me there.

"Get them to the water, Venn," I told him. "I have a plan."

Venn nodded once. I spun around, praying he'd be able to handle himself against them for a minute or two. I ran toward

Sondra, where she was just barely holding off the mongrels surrounding her. Her magic was getting weaker, and the mongrels were closing in on her. I swung my blade outward, cutting three mongrels in one swipe, and jumped over two others until I reached her.

"What will lightning do to vampires?" I asked in a rushed breath.

"With enough power, immobilize them," Sondra answered quickly without looking at me.

"Great. How do I use it?"

The sound of the tiger's growl sounded behind us. *Please be okay, Venn.*

Sondra's gaze flickered to mine before returning to the mongrels in front of us. Sweat dripped down her forehead, and her face had drained of color. She looked on the verge of passing out. "Rae, you're not ready—"

"I am," I argued. At this point, it was do or die. I didn't have a choice.

I glanced behind my shoulder to Venn. The tiger was on top of him, both of them snarling at each other. We didn't have time.

Sondra hesitated before mumbling the incantation for me. "*Fulgur.* Focus the magic in your chest, then shoot it out through your palms."

She quickly demonstrated, but her lightning barely stunned the mongrels.

"*Fulgur...*" I tested the incantation on my tongue. A strong jolt of magic passed through my chest, startling me. I hadn't expected it to feel so powerful. The hairs on my arm rose as the magic passed through my body, but they quickly fell back into place as the magic dissipated. My muscles ached, as if I'd just finished benching a thousand pounds. This spell was not going to go easy on me.

"*Fulgur*," I tried again, this time honing in on that energy and guiding it down my limbs.

Blinding white bolts of lightning shot out of my left palm and connected with at least a dozen mongrels, knocking them off their feet. A deafening *crack* thundered through the cavern, echoing across the lake. Sondra's eyes widened, like she couldn't believe I'd actually done it.

"Get these mongrels into the water," I instructed, trying to mask my exhaustion. "And make sure Venn doesn't die."

Sondra nodded confidently.

I whirled around and shouted across the cavern. "Teagan!"

She kicked a mongrel off Ryland's back while Ryland's teeth sank into the throat of another one. Her eyes darted to mine.

I muttered the incantation again to show her my lightning. I took a chance and directed it toward the tiger shifter. It connected with his chest, stunning him enough that Venn gained the upper hand and sprang to his feet, dodging another spell Witch Guy threw at him. With my eyes on Teagan, I gestured to Venn then to the water. Behind her, Fiona's fox eyes widened in realization, and Teagan's quickly followed. Teagan patted Ryland's back and whispered something in his ear before he took off running toward Witch Guy and the vamp beside him.

I turned to the mongrels and repeated the incantation. I struck five at once, all of which disappeared upon their death. The others shied away, retreating slowly toward the water as I advanced on them on unsteady feet. Ahead of me, Sondra and Witch Guy were battling it out. She shot purple spells at him that looked like fireworks, while he threw green balls of energy back at her. Ryland barreled into the vamp, knocking him backward into the water.

One by one, the mongrels entered the lake, their feet splashing up water at the edge of the shore. One of them in the back must've found a drop-off, because I saw his head bob under the water before he started thrashing around, trying to swim.

Almost there... I gritted my teeth and forced myself to focus past the dizziness assaulting me. I watched the tiger shifter and the Witch Guy closely. All in one moment, the tiger swiped his paw at Venn's face, ripping into the flesh, while Witch Guy's spell finally struck Sondra in the chest. Blood poured from Venn's wound, and Sondra lay motionless on the ground.

The next second, their feet were at the edge of the water. I took my one and only chance and struck.

I never got a chance to see if my lightning hit the water and immobilized them. That last bolt was all my body could take before my knees buckled beneath me and the world faded to black.

23

I blinked my eyes open to a white ceiling. Soft lighting bathed the room. My body felt warm and comfortable, unlike the cool, damp caves we'd been in. My stomach twisted in hunger. Hushed whispers met my ears from across the room. *Venn and Fiona.*

I pushed myself to my elbows to take in more of my surroundings. I saw that I was lying on a queen bed. There was a long dresser on the wall across from me, with a TV on top of it and a desk beside that. The curtains on my left were drawn, but I didn't see any sunlight peeking in around the edges. It must've been late. To my right sat a matching queen bed with someone—I couldn't see who—lying under the covers. Beyond that, a short wall that didn't reach the ceiling separated the bedroom from the rest of the suite. I could hear Venn and Fiona talking from the other side of the divider.

A shadow crossed my bed, and a pair of soft but cold hands touched my shoulder. I leapt in surprise. My eyes darted upward to see Genevieve standing over my bed.

"Lie back," she instructed in a quiet voice. "You need to rest."

I sighed and did as I was told. "What's going on? Is everyone all right? How did we get out of the caves?"

"I think I hear Rae." Fiona's voice came from the other side of the room.

Before Genevieve could answer me, Venn and Fiona popped their heads past the corner of the divider. Half of Venn's face was covered in gauze and tape, but he smiled wide when he saw me. Relief flooded my body, and tears welled in my eyes.

Venn hurried past the other bed to mine. Fiona followed behind him, using a pair of crutches to stabilize herself.

Genevieve stepped aside when Venn reached me. He sat on the side of my bed and leaned down to me. His hands gently touched both sides of my face. I noticed tight gauze wrapping around his hand where the mongrel had bit him. My fingers grazed his good arm, just so I could touch him.

Venn dipped his head and pressed his lips to mine, a full, passionate kiss that sent a warm glow to settle in my chest. He pulled away far too soon.

"What happened?" I asked.

"Your plan worked," Venn answered. "You stunned everyone, and we killed the rest of Matias's men. We got out before any more mongrels attacked."

My head relaxed into the pillow. "How'd we get out? The entrance was blocked."

"There was another exit through the tunnels," Venn said. "Afterward, we called Genevieve. She got on the first plane to Nashville and helped everyone with their injuries. We should all be back to normal soon."

"Where are Teagan and Ryland?" I asked.

"They're fine," Fiona said, sitting down at the end of the bed. "They're bringing back dinner."

"Is Sondra okay?" I glanced to the bed beside mine.

Genevieve nodded. "She's recovering."

"So the spell that hit her…?"

"It was only meant to hurt her," Genevieve answered. "It will pass."

"What happened to everyone while we were separated?" I couldn't keep the questions from tumbling out of my mouth. "I have so much to tell you."

"One second you were there, the next you vanished," Venn told me. "We turned back to go looking for you, but the tunnel led us back to the lake. Then we were attacked."

I furrowed my brow. "How long did it take you to get back?"

Venn shrugged. "Maybe ten minutes."

"No." I shook my head. "I was gone for *hours*."

"The labyrinth screws with your perception of time," Fiona pointed out. "It may very well have been hours, but to us, it was just minutes."

"Matias found me in the caves," I blurted. "He got away with the Artifact. He gave me a blade and said—"

"We know," Fiona interrupted. "Genevieve figured it out when she saw it. You were Elizabeth Martin."

"Yes," I confirmed. "Which means only I can kill Valkas. Where is the dagger?"

Venn shot a glance at Genevieve. *Translation: Genevieve had it.*

My eyes darted between him and Fiona. "We're trusting her now? Like, fully?"

Venn's jaw tensed. "She didn't exactly give us a choice."

"I'm keeping it safe," Genevieve emphasized. "For now."

I lifted my head again, ignoring Venn's hand pushing my shoulder back down to the pillow. "I have to go after him!"

"Yes," Genevieve agreed, "after you rest up."

"No," Venn objected firmly. "You can't go after him."

"What are you talking about?!" I sat straight up, though my head spun. "We're headed to Gregor Island anyway. We know where to find him and have the tools to kill him. We *have* to do this!"

"Going after your sister is one thing," Venn said. "Trying to kill the *original* vampire is another. We'll die before we ever make it close to him."

I crossed my arms. "Are you doubting me? I'm the only person who gets to doubt me, and I'm done with it. I doubted myself as the Ravenite. I doubted myself in the caves. I doubted Synchrony. And I am *done* doubting. I can do this, Venn."

Venn shook his head. "I'm only saying that this is Valkas—"

"And I'm Rachel Collins!" I burst. "I created the damn guy! I need to get rid of him."

"How many lifetimes do you think that will take?" Venn asked rhetorically. "You've already *tried*, Rae. If something happens to you in this life, I wouldn't..." He trailed off.

"This isn't about you," I said sympathetically.

Venn stared back at me, his eyes glistening.

I sighed. "I just mean that this is bigger than any of us. Wouldn't the world be better with the vampires gone? Don't you want revenge on them for changing your brother?"

Venn hesitated, but he didn't get a chance to answer. The hotel room door swung open, and the delicious smell of Chinese takeout hit my nose.

"Dinner!" Ryland called.

"He ate half of it in the car," Teagan teased.

"I had *two* egg rolls!" Ryland clarified.

Fiona rolled her eyes then stood, balancing on her crutches. "You better have saved me a crab rangoon."

"Please," Ryland scoffed as he came into view. "I know better than to eat your food." Ryland's whole body went ridged the second his eyes fell on me.

Teagan appeared behind him, carrying a handful of plastic bags. "Oh, good. Rae's up. See, Ryland? I told you we'd need to order enough for her."

Fiona followed Teagan as she turned to the living area to unpack dinner. Ryland paused for a long moment, crossing his arms and narrowing his gaze at me. I shifted uncomfortably on the bed. What was his problem? Before I could ask, Ryland spun around and disappeared behind the divider.

I looked to Venn for an explanation. "What's up with Ryland?"

Venn hesitated, as if he wasn't sure whether to tell me or not. His shoulders dropped. "He's been acting like that since we learned you were Elizabeth Martin."

I furrowed my brow. "Why? Isn't it good news, since we know how to kill Valkas now?"

Venn chewed on his lower lip. "It is, but... he kind of blames you."

"What?" I asked in disbelief. "But Valkas made me—Elizabeth—do it! He threatened her family... didn't he?"

Venn nodded. "Ryland still says that's no excuse, that because of your decision—Elizabeth's decision—too many people have died. He says she should've chosen the greater good."

"She couldn't have known," I argued.

"I know," Venn said. "We've tried explaining it to him. It's not your fault, Rae. He'll come around eventually."

I groaned. Ryland didn't seem like the kind of guy to *come around* easily. Good thing he didn't know I'd given up The Wise Owl for the dagger; otherwise, he'd be furious at me. I was happy letting him assume Matias got away on his own—and not because of my impulsive decision.

I was starving, so I was going to have to face Ryland sooner than later. I started to get up, but Genevieve flicked her finger from the foot of my bed. An invisible force held me in place.

Holy crap! This lady had some serious magical skills.

"Stay," she instructed. "You need to rest. I will bring you some food."

Her hold on me vanished, and I relaxed back into the pillow.

"Dibs on an eggroll," I called after her before turning my attention back to Venn. "So, about Valkas?"

Venn's jaw clenched. "This isn't up for discussion."

My jaw dropped. "Who died and made you the boss of me?"

Venn took a deep breath and ran his fingers through his hair, the muscles in his biceps rippling. "I'm not trying to tell you what to do—"

"But you are!" I accused.

"I'm just trying to keep you from making a stupid decision."

I almost snapped back, until he pulled me into his arms. My head lay against his chest. I felt so warm and comfortable. It was like waking up in heaven. How could I argue with him when he felt this great?

"I care about you, Rae," he said softly, placing a kiss on the top of my head. Tingles spread down my body. "I don't want you getting hurt."

I ran the palm of my hand up his arm, enjoying the goose-bumps that traveled along my own skin. "I don't want to hurt you, either."

It was the truth. As I said it, the strongest sense of guilt assaulted my gut, immediately masking any appetite I thought I had. Bile rose in my throat.

It didn't matter what Venn said or how much I cared for him. Once I was back on my feet, I was going to Gregor Island... with or without him.

That's where I'd finally find Jenna—and where I'd kill Valkas.

END OF BOOK TWO

Continue the series in book three, *Resolute*.

ABOUT THE AUTHOR

Alicia Rades is a USA Today bestselling author of young adult and new adult paranormal fiction. When she's not dreaming up magical stories, she's either binge-watching paranormal TV shows, meditating, or spending time with her family. She has an unhealthy obsession with psychic characters and writes with a deck of tarot cards next to her computer.